The Last Egyptian Mamluk

Joyce Anne Nicholls

The Last Egyptian Mamluk

For information about special discounts for bulk purchases, please contact Sunbury Press, Inc. Wholesale Dept. at (717) 254-7274 or orders@sunburypress.com.

To request one of our authors for speaking engagements or book signings, please contact Sunbury Press, Inc. Publicity Dept. at publicity@sunburypress.com.

FIRST SUNBURY PRESS EDITION
Printed in the United States of America
January 2012

Trade Paperback ISBN: 978-1-62006-004-9
Mobipocket format (Kindle) ISBN: 978-1- 62006-005-6
ePub format (Nook) ISBN: 978-1-62006-006-3

Published by:
Sunbury Press
Camp Hill, PA
www.sunburypress.com

Camp Hill, Pennsylvania   USA

For my sons, Allan and Christopher, who have always believed in me, my grandchildren Shayna (who worked on the cover art), Caelan and Sahara, my parents, Alroy and Sylvia Nicholls, who would have been so proud, and my siblings, relatives and friends. Thanks for your love and encouragement.

1

Alexandria, 1775

Qilij wrapped his blanket tightly around him to ward off the chill. Night had fallen but he refused to sleep in the wakalah with the merchants in spite of its central location in the bazaar because the noisy bargaining could sometimes go on all night. The rooms were always quickly filled. After days on the move the traders welcomed the opportunity to have a roof over their heads, cooked meals and a safe place to store the goods they had brought to sell. But Qilij preferred to sleep outdoors. The traders had come from afar and their only mode of transportation was by camel. But after weeks, sometimes even months of journeying through the desert in the excessive heat, the pungent odour of camel combined with human sweat and the smell of the dye emanating from their unwashed clothing was intolerable. Outdoors, surrounded by his personal bodyguard in case he was attacked by a rival mamluk faction, Qilij would at least be able to breathe. He closed his eyes but sleep failed to come.

He had arrived in Alexandria almost a week ago to purchase some Arabian horses and would be returning to Cairo on the morrow. After the showings he had selected three fine steeds, one a mare, and expected to conclude the purchase before noon. Still, he knew the reason why sleep was eluding him had nothing to do with the horses. It was the slave boy that was keeping him awake.

Apparently the boy was part of the trader's caravan but anyone blessed with eyesight could see he was in no way related to the trader. Apart from the fact that their skin colour was nearly identical there was no familial resemblance whatsoever between them. Moreover, the trader's eyes were brown whereas the boy's were blue. He wore a kufiyyah, a head wrap probably given to him by the trader to protect his head from the sun but some of his

1

hair had escaped and tumbled about his ears. It was light-coloured, no doubt bleached by the same scorching desert sun that had darkened his skin before the trader took pity on him.

It was almost a certainty that the boy was one of the pathetic raggle-taggle band of Russian children who, rejected as being too young for the mamluk army, had been abandoned by the desperate parents who had brought them to the slave market to sell. Alone and destitute, they roamed the cities in bands, living by their wits in the alleyways in the daytime and sleeping in whatever shelter they could find outside the city walls at night, until they either died of disease or starvation, were killed by marauding bedouins or were captured and carted away to be sold into slavery elsewhere.

It was obvious why the trader kept the boy around. He had a knack with horses that seemed almost uncanny. Over the past few days Qilij's eyes had followed him as he raced the horses bareback around the camp demonstrating their form. Despite his servitude and his small size, there was something defiant and proud in his bearing as he sat firmly astride the horse, seeming almost a part of the animal. But Qilij knew that if by some misfortune he should suffer a fall and break a bone, the trader would move on without him; leave him to die like a dog in the desert.

Still, the boy would consider himself lucky, despite the fact that life as he knew it most likely consisted of daily abuse and cuffs to the head, barely enough to eat and overwork under the endless assault of heat, sand and flies. But having an owner meant he was protected from those who would have murdered him merely because, in their eyes, he had no right to exist.

He looked to be about six or seven years old but might well have been older, his growth stunted owing to lack of proper food and care. Whatever the reason for his diminutive size, it was unlikely that he would be of any real use for some time. Taking him back to Cairo would simply mean an extra mouth to feed, another addition to a household which already included a harem of two women, Qilij's natural son, a boy of five whose mother had died giving birth to him, and the mamluks who were still under his patronage.

Qilij al-Kvareli was an amir who had enjoyed a successful military career, rising from the rank of soldier to commander of forty mamluks. During that time he had managed to acquire significant personal wealth through his own efforts as mamluks were expected to do. Now retired from active service he could still afford a lavish lifestyle and to indulge in luxuries such as fine horses. Which was what he had come to Alexandria to do, Qilij reminded himself. Buying a young slave who wouldn't even be capable of earning his keep for years had definitely not been part of the plan.

He must have drifted off because when next Qilij opened his eyes a new day had dawned and he realized that somehow, even as he slept, he had come to a decision. At first the trader demurred, claiming the boy's knack with the horses was of great value to him, so much so that despite his small size he had in jest named him Maxim, the great one, as a sort of homage to the extraordinary talent that resided in such a small body. But when Qilij appeared to lose interest in buying the horses he capitulated and accepted Qilij's offer for the boy. The caravan would depart day after tomorrow and he dared not risk losing such a good sale or, for that matter, his life. Mamluks did not take kindly to losing. In anything.

2.

Cairo

Three days later Qilij returned from Alexandria to his home in Cairo with the skinny ragged urchin in tow. He ordered the servants to take him to the bath house and clean him up. The boy emerged about half an hour later, a shade or two lighter now that the dirt and grime embedded in his skin had been washed away. He was dressed in some clothes that one of Qilij's mamluks had outgrown, and his hair had been cut to get rid of lice. The roots showed that its natural colour was light brown and that it had a tendency to curl.

He was taken to the kitchen and given some food which he devoured hastily, as if in fear it would be taken away before he was finished. His expression was wary, as though suspicious of such good fortune. It was weeks before he stopped bolting his food. The first few nights he slept sitting up, wrapped in his bedroll with his back against the wall. After several nights, his suspicions apparently allayed since no harm had yet befallen him, he allowed himself to stretch out full length on the luxurious carpets.

In the beginning he was left to his own devices, to wander about the compound quietly absorbing a way of life that nothing in his experience would have given him the capacity to even imagine. He kept to himself but gradually became a regular visitor to the stables where he would help groom horses, other than those of the mamluks. The grooms had warned him that a mamluk had complete responsibility for the care of his horse and allowed no one else to touch it.

From the very first day five-year old Arun, Qilij's natural son, had begun following him around. After a while, it was normal to see them together and the fact that

Maxim, as everyone now called him, was older seemed to
make no difference. They became inseparable: eating,
sleeping and playing together. It was evident that Arun
idolized Maxim and that Maxim had slipped into the role of
older brother and looked out for Arun.

Then one day Qilij returned home with two fine new
horses. One was for Maxim, the other for Arun. Somewhere
along the line it had become an unwritten rule that only
mamluks or those in training could go about Cairo on
horseback, but Qilij had apparently decided to ignore it. As
a precaution he warned them to remain inside the
compound, at least until they were older.

The look on Maxim's face as he swung himself into the
saddle of his very own horse was one that would forever
stay with Qilij. He remained stationary in the saddle for
several moments, his hand stroking the horse's long
elegant neck while he talked softly to it. Then abruptly, he
got off the horse, walked up to Qilij and stood there,
looking up at him uncertainly. Divining from the
expression in the boy's eyes what he wanted to say, Qilij
leaned over slightly and put his arms around him
awkwardly. He surprised himself not a little since he was
not a man given to displays of affection.

It was the first time in Maxim's short and hitherto
miserable existence that he recalled being touched
affectionately by another human being and he felt a
strangeness inside his chest, as though something were
trying to burst out of it. In that moment Maxim's love for
Qilij was born. Shortly after, he began to address Qilij as
father, just as Arun did. It felt odd on his tongue at first
and he used the word tentatively, testing it almost. But
gradually, with repetition, it began to feel right because the
bond between them was as deep as that of a loving father
and son. Secure in the love and affection of his father and
brother, Maxim's secret misgiving—that his wonderful new
life was really a dream from which he would awaken one
morning and find himself back in the desert with the
trader's caravan—gradually subsided.

3

Now that Maxim's mind was at ease his body seemed to follow suit and began to fill out. At first, most likely because he saw Maxim every day, Qilij did not notice the changes. But then one day, as he observed Maxim on his horse, Qilij realized with a small sense of surprise that the boy seemed to have developed into a muscular teenager practically overnight and, what was more, he seemed to have honed the ability he had displayed when Qilij first laid eyes on him and had become a talented horseman. In fact, in all his years of recruiting and training young mamluks, Qilij had never seen one whose destiny seemed so apparent. There was no question in Qilij's mind, no time to lose. Maxim would have to begin his training as a mamluk soldier immediately.

Qilij knew just where he would place the boy for his training. Many years ago, he and three other amirs had jointly purchased some land on the outskirts of the city and developed it for their use in training their own mamluks. But this was an activity he had long since put behind him and truth be told, he had no desire to resume it. He and his business partners had all retired but they had retained ownership of the facility, which they now leased to other senior mamluks who still purchased and trained mamluks. Fortunately, mamluks were now free to do as they pleased, live where they wanted, just as long as they were prepared to serve in the sultan's army in wartime. There would be no difficulty arranging for Maxim to join one of the groups currently being trained at the facility. As well, even though Qilij himself was now too old to participate in the actual exercises, it was an additional advantage that his financial interest in the facility would give him access to observe and to be vigilant regarding all aspects of Maxim's training.

4

Watching from the sidelines at the training field it was clear to Qilij that he had been absolutely right. Maxim was destined to be a mamluk. He was imbued with a passion for excellence. He would spend hours tirelessly honing his skills with the lance, the sword, the bow and the mace, acquitting himself well in drills when he would compete against other young mamluks like himself. To round out the trainees' education time was set aside each day for study of the teachings and practices of Islam and in this Maxim excelled as well. He seemed driven by an overwhelming desire to please his father and had confided to Qilij his personal ambition to excel at everything.

The one drawback to his training—and privately Maxim no longer considered it as such—was that he did not experience the feelings of true brotherhood with the other soldiers that was a fundamental characteristic of mamluks. The bond that existed among mamluks was second only to their deep loyalty and attachment to their benefactors but it was a bond that was normally cemented during training. It was an attachment that would endure on and off the battlefield despite the ever-present unspoken understanding that if an opportunity presented itself to seize the wealth of another, all bets would be off. It was their way of life.

In the beginning Maxim had been conscious of feeling a bit different from the other trainees, of not really being one of them. It worried him a little until one day comprehension dawned. Without Arun most likely he would have felt that nothing could surpass the closeness he felt towards the group. But that was because there would have been nowhere else to look for sibling companionship. But he, Maxim, already had what the other trainees were seeking in each other: he had a brother. So it was not a question of not belonging after all.

7

Friendship and love of a brother were two different things
and had it not been for Qilij and Arun, he would never
have known the difference or understood that something
very important in his life was lacking.

After working all that out on his own Maxim no longer
wondered about his relationship with his fellow trainees.
As far as he was concerned it was precisely what it was
supposed to be.

Arun had done some thinking as well. One of the things
that bothered him was his height. He was shorter than
Maxim and had decided it was not only because he was
younger. He had been doing his stretching exercises
faithfully for almost a year, ever since he realized that his
growth seemed to be slowing down. Perhaps it was time to
admit that it might have stopped altogether and that he
was now as tall as he would ever be?

When Arun looked in the mirror the face that looked
back at him might well have been that of a young girl. The
one redeeming masculine feature of his face that he could
point to were his eyebrows, which were thick and bushy.
And totally incongruous over those big brown eyes that
said to the world that their owner couldn't—and

wouldn't—hurt a fly. Was it possible that fate had made
a mistake in making him a boy? No. Not possible, Arun
decided. This was just the way it was, who he was
supposed to be.

Arun thought the world of Maxim but he himself had
no desire whatsoever to be a soldier and was thankful that
he could never be a mamluk; it would have forced him to
make soldiering his career. Nor was he particularly
interested in becoming a dedicated scholar. He was a
dreamer, content to let Maxim be the one to excel in those
military skills that, as was becoming clearer with each
passing day, would soon mark him as a formidable soldier.

He felt not the slightest concern about disappointing
his father, knowing full well that nothing would be
expected of him apart perhaps from supervising his
father's tax collectors when he was old enough to
undertake that task. His mother had died giving birth to
him. If she had lived she would have assumed the status of

8

first wife in the harem, not that it would have made any difference to Arun's future. He had no birthright, no legal claim to Qilij's property. Nor did Maxim, for that matter. The mamluks' strength was predicated on being a one-generation aristocracy, meaning that their property could not be inherited. Should Maxim wish to hold on to Qilij's property after the latter passed away, he would have to be ready to defend it from potential usurpers—other mamluks who were always on the lookout for opportunities to increase their wealth. Arun was well aware that Qilij was preparing Maxim for this inevitable challenge and he was confident that when Maxim's destiny came looking for him, it would find him ready.

5

1791

Arun opened his eyes to see Maxim's anxious face looming over him.

"Idiot," Maxim said, sounding disgusted. "You let that serpent Khalid creep up on you through the bushes. He must have followed us out of the city. If something hadn't told me to come back and look for you, you would be food for the jackals by now."

Maxim stood up, thrusting his sabre back into its sheath. "Here," he said, holding out his hand.

Arun grasped it and pulled himself to his feet. He wasn't fooled by Maxim's show of disgust. They had been close since childhood, as close as if they had been blood brothers.

"Did he at least feel the sting of your sword?" Arun asked.

"No. He slithered away into the bushes like the loathsome viper that he is, so I could not follow him. Besides, I wanted to see if you were still alive or not. He dropped his dagger," Maxim added. He held it aloft, regarding the jewelled handle with satisfaction. "He seemed about to slit your throat."

"He sought only to frighten me. He taunted me that I should hide my face behind the veil because it was the face of a woman," Arun said ruefully.

"Do you not know that the real reason he hates you is because the fair Zainab finds you too beautiful?" Maxim inquired, his eyes sparkling merrily.

"She loves you and well you know it, dolt," Arun said, cuffing Maxim lightly on the side of his head. "She makes eyes at me to make you jealous and Khalid the fool, who does not even suspect her true feelings, thinks I am his rival."

At this, Maxim threw his head back and guffawed. His laughter was infectious and Arun's eyes rested on his face with amused affection. This brother of his could easily have been mistaken for a soldier of fortune. His hair, light brown and curling, had escaped from the yellow bandanna tied around his forehead (it was too hot for a turban, he said) and tumbled down to his shoulders. Since it was an abysmally hot summer, he had adopted a daring style of dress on his days off. He was wearing the voluminous pantalons favoured by his caste, the mamluks, but instead of the usual long robe he had substituted a fine, white muslin shirt with long sleeves, over which he wore a waist-length, richly embroidered sleeveless jacket of bright red satin, and his feet were encased in soft red boots with silver spurs. He embodied a youthful free-spiritedness that was completely engaging.

"Perhaps you should consider becoming a suitor for the hand of Zainab," Maxim said merrily. "Since it seems you are going to be blamed by Khalid in any case, it would be less of an injustice if you had indeed gotten something in exchange. I fancy that if she had the choice, she would not choose Khalid for her husband."

"I would still be her second choice," Arun replied, "even though it would be of no importance to me that you were first in her heart. But I have made it known that I do not wish to marry. Her aunt, the betrother, who knows I am of marriageable age even though my face is as yet hairless, has already approached me and offered to find me a suitable wife."

"It will soon be rumoured that you are a very strange and unnatural fellow for an Egyptian. One who is not called to be a holy man and yet refuses to take a wife. You do not even belong to the Brotherhood," Maxim observed.

"I admire some of the teachings of the Sufis," Arun admitted, "but I do not think I am capable of making the necessary sacrifices and giving up things in life that I find enjoyable. Yet, when I look beyond Cairo, to the desert, where the pyramids reach upward to Allah, I am entranced. This is how I achieve my oneness with Him. I do not achieve my dhikr with prayers and incantations." He paused, a mischievous smile hovering on his lips. "But in case you think I still sound too self-absorbed, I must confess why I am unlikely to join the Brotherhood. My reason is very, very practical," he ended, grinning.

Maxim regarded him suspiciously: "And what is that?"

"The truth is I could not wear their woollen garment. Wool makes me itch," he said, and they both burst out laughing.

"Still, I am glad you have not joined the Brotherhood," Maxim confessed, after their laughter subsided. "Little by little it is becoming the religion of the peasants, full of superstition and ignorance. Even though you are half Egyptian, you have been so well educated by our father that you will never be one of the masses. And I am glad of that."

"I am grateful to our father for all that he has given me," Arun said. "But I am neither one of you, nor am I truly Egyptian. In truth, I belong nowhere, so I am worse off than the fellahin."

He gestured towards a group of peasants walking single file in the distance. "They at least know they belong here."

Maxim's face stiffened as his eyes followed the peasants. Centuries of mamluk distrust of the Egyptian peasant was the legacy that had been passed down to him by his benefactor, the man whom he called father.

"Perhaps they do," he replied dryly. "But I wager that not a single one would hesitate to change places with you, had he but the chance."

He glanced around, suddenly uneasy. He had learned early on that the fellahin could not be trusted. They lied about the true amount of their produce, hoping to reduce the taxes they paid in exchange for being allowed to cultivate the land. It was necessary to deal harshly with the cheaters once they were discovered, to make examples of them. Barefooted and dressed in rags, eyes downcast, they appeared harmless enough. But the mamluks knew that deep anger and resentment toward their masters always lay just below the surface and it had boiled over in the past. Each revolt had been swiftly and ruthlessly put down, but Maxim had heard his father say a mamluk landowner would be foolhardy to turn his back on a peasant, or ride about the countryside alone.

The sun was sinking in the west, bathing the skies in a golden haze that deepened over the desert and poured down upon it like a solid sheet of amber rain. The stillness was beginning to feel oppressive. The large sycamore, whose wide-spread branches had invited Arun to linger in its shade, now seemed vaguely threatening; its gnarled trunk like some twisted Pandora's Box, waiting for the cover of darkness to release its ugly secrets.

Maxim was neither superstitious nor fanciful, but he had learned to trust his instincts. He whistled to his horse grazing nearby and it trotted obediently up to him, followed closely by Arun's horse. He seized the bridle and swung himself into the saddle.

His urgency communicated itself to Arun, who lost no time in following his lead. With a harmony born of years of riding together they spurred the horses lightly, racing out of the grove and up onto the embankment, stirring up a cloud of dust that would mark their passage all the way to Cairo.

They had followed the Nile a great distance from the city, perhaps too far. By the time they returned it would be past sundown and they would have missed the last call to prayer. But neither one considered for a moment stopping en route to pray and they barely noticed the villagers kneeling in the dust along the embankment, their faces turned to Mecca.

6

Night had fallen by the time the two boys regained the outskirts of Cairo but they just made it through the city gates before they closed. Once inside the city walls they slowed the horses to a trot, guiding them through the maze of narrow unpaved alleyways. The merchants had already shut their shops for the night and the streets were dark and deserted. At nightfall Cairenes hastened to the refuge of their homes. The only people about were the sentinels who watched over the city at night and the porters hired by the mamluk elite and by the wealthy Egyptians to stand guard at their gates.

As Maxim and Arun approached the Kvareli house, which was situated in the mamluk quarter, the clatter of the horses' hooves on the cobblestones awakened the night porter. He tumbled off the makeshift cot where he had been dozing instead of keeping watch and rushed to open the gate. They dismounted, throwing the reins to the little groom trotting behind the porter and followed the passage that led to the inner courtyard.

The entrance to the house was modest, like most of the grand houses in Cairo. It was hardly more than an opening in the wall, a style borrowed from the Egyptians who had learned the hard way that a display of wealth would inevitably provoke the unwanted attention of the mamluks, who considered luxury and elegance their exclusive preserve and would not hesitate to acquire, usually by force, anything that suited their fancy. The modest tunnel-like entrance gave no indication of the splendour that lay behind it, affording its owners a degree of protection from their own kind, rival mamluk factions against whom they were constantly engaged in a struggle for wealth and power.

"It seems that our father has visitors," Arun murmured as they entered the courtyard. Several mamluk soldiers were standing around, conversing with one another, but Maxim did not know any of them well. He entered the courtyard and a little silence fell as they turned toward him, their expressions watchful, determining whether the newcomer might be friend or foe. Aware of what lay behind their scrutiny Maxim raised his hand in a brief but friendly gesture. Recognizing him they returned his greeting in similar fashion and resumed their conversation, but now their voices were more muted. Maxim continued across the courtyard, conscious that their new topic of conversation was likely none other than himself and his future prospects.

Qilij had devoted considerable time and resources to Maxim's training and his intention could not have been more transparent. He had prepared the boy to take control of his benefactor's wealth and property and to defend it against would-be usurpers who would be breaking down the gates to seize it by brute force once Qilij passed on. Already Qilij could see the speculation in the eyes of his compatriots when they looked at Maxim. Being a mamluk himself, albeit retired, it would have never occurred to him to question their right to challenge Maxim. In their place he would have acted exactly the same because mamluks were first and foremost a master race of soldiers. They expected their leaders to earn the right to lead and to be accepted as leader by demonstrating not only military prowess and superiority but the power to acquire wealth in their own right. It was the only way to guarantee their race would remain strong. A life of ease effortlessly acquired could only make a man soft, unfit for battle, unfit to lead. Without an inheritance to look forward to, the only path to enrichment for a mamluk was by a show of strength, be it usurpation or murder. If Maxim lacked the strength to repel his attackers, he would have little chance of holding on to what was his.

Maxim and Arun crossed the courtyard, pausing briefly to refresh themselves at the fountain before ascending the short flight of stairs that led to the main floor, the street side of which featured a passage enclosed on both sides with intricately carved mashrabiya. While allowing fresh air to circulate, the mashrabiya screened the women of the household if they wished to look out, keeping them secure in the knowledge that they themselves were all but invisible to anyone on the outside looking in.

"I will leave you to enjoy the company of soldiers," Arun said, smiling. "Sleep well, my brother." They embraced and Arun disappeared into the left wing of the house where the men's rooms were located. Maxim headed down the short passage on the right that would take him into the mandara where his father customarily received guests.

As he approached, the sweetish smell of the smoke from a waterpipe wafting into the corridor seeped into Maxim's nostrils and gave him a very good idea as to the identity of his father's guests.

Kurjii al-Saleh would be there, Maxim knew. Kurjii was the sole mamluk, besides himself, that his father felt he could trust. The two had come up through the ranks together, beginning as slave boys. They had used their military prowess to strengthen their hold on the wealth they had managed to acquire and both had become very rich. Their elegant lifestyles were paid for with taxes collected from the fellahin who cultivated the land for them, just as their predecessors had done. They moved about Cairo protected by their mamluks and attended by a retinue of slaves. These two symbols testified to their status as amirs and therefore in need of constant protection.

Baltaa al-Ashraf would be there also. He would be the one smoking the waterpipe. He was a quiet and intense man but the fire of ambition burned in his brown eyes, contrasting oddly with his calm expression and the softness of his voice. Its pitch remained constant even when others around him erupted into voluble eloquence. Baltaa, everyone knew, was constantly alert for new opportunities to increase his wealth. But outside of the ones he created, whether by force or by treachery, new opportunities were rare. So he would wait, ready to seize any opening, to pounce at the slightest sign of weakness. On more than one occasion Maxim had been conscious of being keenly scrutinized by Baltaa. He was well aware that behind that calm façade Baltaa was assessing, weighing, calculating—already pitting his strength against Maxim, who had begun to show signs that he would know how to seize power and repulse attempts to wrest it away from him.

Sanjar al-Zahir and Qarat al-Madari were likely among his father's visitors as well. Similar in rank to Baltaa they nonetheless deferred to him in unspoken acknowledgement that barring some untimely event, he would be the first to gain ascendancy.

And yet, even as they dreamed and schemed and plotted against each other, a strange kind of solidarity united them, as it did with all the mamluks, allowing them to quickly close ranks against any outsider who threatened a way of life that had survived five hundred years of assault from the enemy outside and from the even more ruthless enemy within, other mamluk factions.

7

As Maxim entered the mandara he saw that the visitors were precisely who he had guessed they might be. Their murmured conversation died away as he entered the room and he experienced yet again that familiar sensation of heightened awareness, an overall sense of needing to be prepared that Baltaa's presence always brought.

The room exuded the refinement and splendour that, over the centuries, had become second nature to the mamluks. The dim lighting from the oil lamps served only to enhance the atmosphere of softness and luxury created by the richness of the furnishings. Thick Persian carpets covered the floor, their shade and texture softening the transition from its hard neutral stone to the exotic patterns of the glazed Turkish tiles that lined the walls in cobalt blue to a height of about four feet. Deep within each tile the flickering light from the lamps hanging in each corner of the room danced like stardust trapped inside the night sky. The delicate lattice of the mashrabiya stretched upwards like a panel of lace, leading the eye to the intricate patterns adorning the domed ceiling. The remaining wall space was covered with tapestries and shelves displaying exquisite objets d'art and delicate Chinese porcelain. On the floor, ivory and ebony sculptures stood among huge vases and bowls made of pottery, brass and copper, creating three-dimensional still lifes. A statuesque Ethiopian slave attended each corner.

Maxim crossed the room to where his father sat on a divan strewn with Turkish carpets. Embracing his father he sank down cross legged on the floor near the divan and faced the visitors.

Baltaa removed the jewelled ivory mouthpiece of his waterpipe from his mouth and fixed his bright eyes on Maxim's face.

"Perhaps this young fellow has some news from the streets," he suggested.

"No news except that which was all over Cairo this morning," Maxim replied. "Every townsman and villager now knows that the sultan has pardoned Murad and Ibrahim Bey and that they have since returned to Cairo."

"We have been speaking of this," Qilij replied. "It seems that the two have reason to be grateful to the plague which has gripped Cairo since the new year began. With the Ottoman regime practically wiped out, including Ismael Bey himself, there was no one left to prevent them from entering the city."

"And they have wasted no time," Kurjii interjected, his voice betraying anger. "Already they have begun making demands, levying heavy additional taxes indiscriminately. It seems no one will escape their greed. No one!"

"They appear to have picked up where they left off five years ago, just before the pasha kicked them out of Cairo in 1786," Baltaa said mildly.

"Apparently he did not kick them far enough, only into Upper Egypt," Sanjar commented, smiling sardonically.

"And even then, it was not long before they were controlling vast areas well beyond their appointed districts," Baltaa replied.

Maxim, who had been following their conversation keenly, glanced quickly at Baltaa. Something in Baltaa's voice resonated unpleasantly in Maxim's ears and he realized instantly that in his heart Baltaa admired Murad and Ibrahim Bey, the ruthless and power-hungry duo whose greed and aggression had brought about economic chaos in Cairo before the Ottoman government finally stepped in. Maxim turned to look at his father but Qilij's eyes were on Baltaa and Maxim knew, from his father's set expression that he, too, had discerned Baltaa's true feelings.

"They are predators." Qilij pronounced. "They act jointly when they find it convenient to do so, but they have turned against each other many times before and will again. But whether acting jointly or separately, they share a single goal: to enrich themselves at any cost. Regardless of which one prevails, Cairo, nay, the whole of Egypt will be a hundred times worse off before they are done."

"How so?" Baltaa inquired challengingly.

"Because now they will also seek revenge. Do you not recall that when he sent them into Upper Egypt, the pasha had seized all their property and the property and jewels of their wives as well, to compensate for the required payments they had withheld from Istanbul for many years? They were left with nothing and it is a certainty that even after they have recouped every last dirhem that was taken from them, their insatiable demands will not cease."

"Yes, I do recall," Baltaa acknowledged. "The pasha also appropriated the property of their wealthier mamluks as well. At the time I did think he might have gone a bit too far when he ordered that the mamluks' wives and concubines be auctioned off."

A brief silence ensued, conveying what might have been tacit agreement with Baltaa's view that the pasha might indeed have gone too far.

"All the same," Qilij said into the silence, "the return of the two could not have come at a worse time. We landowners will not escape their grasp. They will increase the tribute levels and since the fellahin are incapable of doing more, it will have to come out of our own purses. It comforts me not at all to know that the taxes we pay will never find their way to Istanbul. They will only enrich the coffers of Murad and Ibrahim Bey." Bitterness tinged his voice.

Baltaa drew on his mouthpiece and puffed the smoke out from the sides of his mouth.

"You are becoming soft with old age, my friend," he proffered at last. "I for one am not convinced that the fellahin would be unable to pay more taxes. They cheat and lie about the amount of their produce as you well know."

"If old age brings the wisdom to understand that blood cannot be wrung out of a stone, then I welcome it," Qilij retorted, his tone becoming acerbic. "Low Niles and food shortages brought on by the never-ending internal conflicts that disrupt the safe passage of goods in transit have hit the fellahin hard. They are unable to withstand the effects of the plague which has hovered over Egypt these many years and have been dropping like flies. Their animals, too. We cannot bury our heads in the sand and pretend that nothing has changed for the fellahin. But even if that were the case," he concluded, "it seems to me that if they lie and cheat, they have learned well from their masters."

"This seems strange talk from the lips of one who in the past has had to punish the fellahin for cheating," Qarat said. Maxim noticed that his eyes never seemed to be entirely focused on any one object or person, making him appear perpetually distracted.

"I understand it but that does not mean I condone it," Qilij replied, somewhat sharply. "The point is that we have already paid our fair share of tribute. If we try to raise more by increasing the tax on the peasants who have long been in dire straits they will simply give up what is already a futile struggle and leave their villages. What will we do then? Pay our soldiers more to find them and force them back to work even though they are ailing? In my opinion that would be akin to throwing our money to the four winds."

"Your point is well made," Baltaa conceded, "and I will think further on it. But for now it has been a long day and I must bid you good night." He laid his mouthpiece on the edge of the brass bowl next to his waterpipe and rose to his feet.

"May Allah watch over you in sleep," he said. He glanced at Maxim, his eyes shrewd and penetrating. "And you also, Maxim."

As if it had been a signal they all got to their feet. Qilij moved from one to the other, embracing each in turn. A servant materialized with a lighted lamp and they followed him out.

Qilij and Maxim remained silent until the clattering of horses' hooves signalled that their visitors were on their way out of the compound.

"Your views will be known all over the city by noon tomorrow, father," Maxim burst out. He was more than a little fearful that perhaps Qilij had been too frank.

Qilij smiled. "Then I will have succeeded in my intention," he said. "Baltaa has the soul of a traitor. He will carry the message I wanted him to carry to the beys of the governing council. I have spoken for the majority of the landowners. There are a few thousand of us but only twenty-three beys. They would be wise not to press us too hard since it is with our strength that they govern."

He put his arms around Maxim and embraced him. "I will bid you goodnight, Maxim. I am in need of softer company. Probably a consequence of spending the entire evening with soldiers," he added. He sounded weary.

Maxim would have cut out his tongue before saying anything that might have sounded even remotely critical of his benefactor. Privately, however, he felt that the harem weakened a soldier, made him soft. Maxim had never considered marriage, even though the old crone had also offered to find him a wife. Suddenly, however, he was glad that the two women of the harem would see to his father's comfort, because it was clear that Qilij was feeling his age and would soon need more care.

"Good night, my father," he said, returning Qilij's embrace. "Sleep well."

Maxim beckoned to the slave who came forward carrying one of the oil lamps.

"My father wishes to go upstairs," he said.

As Qilij followed the slave up the stairs Maxim observed how the latter moved deliberately, pausing for a moment on each step so that he was never more than one step ahead of his master. All the while he held the lamp up high so that the entire staircase above and below Qilij was illuminated. It occurred to Maxim that the slave was more attuned to his father's needs and the state of his health than he was. He felt a twinge of guilt but managed to suppress his sudden impulse to rush up the stairs and take his father's arm, help him up. Qilij was a proud man and a mamluk. He would not want to be reminded, even by his son, that he was now an old man.

8

Murad and Ibrahim Bey buried their aggression towards each other once more and exercised a dual governorship over Egypt. But it was an uneasy truce. Behind the scenes, knowing their duumvirate was tenuous, the two were engaged in a fierce struggle to gain the ascendancy, seeking supporters among the beys of the governing council by paying them enormous bribes in the form of lands and money. In the meantime, they ruled their lesser subjects ruthlessly, handing down sentences of flogging and sometimes death for even minor infractions or disobedience, depending heavily on an army of a mere fifteen thousand soldiers to control the population of some three million people, the majority of whom were peasants.

Life for the peasants had become more miserable than ever. In addition to the plague, the water levels of the Nile had remained low over the past few years and crop failure high, due to the dryness of the soil. In some parts, the delta had become little more than a dust bowl. Inflation was running high and those who had barely existed at subsistence levels before, were now sliding into abject poverty. Entire families of peasants had given up the struggle and were now begging in the streets of Cairo. Slum communities were springing up literally overnight, even in the courtyards of the mosques, and outbreaks of plague were frequent.

Ignoring the misery all around them, the beys continued to exact higher and higher levels of tribute from the landowners to support their lavish lifestyles and to pay for the bribes they dispensed. Most of the landowners then turned around and applied equal pressure on the fellahin to prevent a drop in the standard of living to which they themselves had grown accustomed. As Qilij had prophesied, many of the fellahin who had remained on the land were now simply walking away, abandoning their villages and fields to join their brethren in one or other of the burgeoning slum communities in the city.

Maxim and Arun had remained as close as they had been in their youth. Neither one had married. Maxim had completed his training some years ago and been formally manumitted by his benefactor who was Qilij. He now carried out his duties as one of Qilij's mamluks. Arun had taken charge of the accounts and the entire household relied on him to ensure that money was available to meet all their needs. Qilij, in failing health, appeared content with the arrangement, especially since it freed him to enjoy more relaxing pursuits.

Discipline among mamluk soldiers had become a serious problem, since some of the younger ones were quick to realize that their efforts were making their leaders even richer, while luxuries for themselves were few and far between. Reports of whole villages being sacked by mamluks were coming in daily. They stole everything and anything of even the most trifling value, shot the peasants, raped their daughters and burned whole villages down before they left.

Maxim listened to these stories with dismay. He did not doubt for one moment that they were true. He only had to look around him for confirmation. What he saw were soldiers who had become coarse and slack in their habits, their morals and their dress: a slipshod bunch of men unfit and unready for duty. With each passing day they grew lazier and lazier, frequenting the brothels which had sprung up in Cairo, where a young boy or a girl could be had for a few dirhems; they were interested only in working less, but for more pay.

Even before he had begun his training Maxim's dream was to become a real soldier: to fight in a real war. His training finally complete, he was more resolved than ever that when that day came he would be ready. But now it seemed that the dream was collapsing all around him.

"You seem distracted," Qilij remarked to Maxim one night. Maxim and Arun had joined him for coffee after they had eaten their evening meal.

"Yes," Arun observed, looking at Maxim perplexedly. "What is the matter with you? You have hardly said two words all evening."

"That's because there is no need for me to talk. You have enough to say for the two of us," Maxim replied with a grin. "I'm sorry, father," he continued, turning to Qilij. "Lately, all I seem able to think about is whether I will still have a career in five years' time. The way things are going now with our soldiers if there is ever another war few of them will be in any shape to fight it. We will have to look to the Turkish janissaries to do the fighting for us, although they seem to have become as undisciplined as the mamluks," he concluded.

"Well, do you have a solution, other than complaining about it?" Qilij inquired.

"No," Maxim admitted. "What can I do? I am just one soldier, and a very junior one at that. I cannot fix the whole army," he added, sounding a little defensive.

"No, you can't," Arun said soothingly. "But maybe you can fix your own corner of it."

"What are you talking about?" Maxim demanded, a trifle irritably.

Qilij's eyes moved interestedly from one son to the other, but he remained silent.

"Well, if you want to be a soldier and to make that your career, then let it be on your own terms. Be choosy about the soldiers with whom you spend your time. Surround yourself with those who think like you, who share your goals and are also ambitious," Arun advised him

"That is harder to do than you imagine," Maxim replied. "Even if I could find some, right now I don't have time to go looking for friends. I spend most of my days with father's other mamluks, patrolling his land to ensure that the peasants are left in peace to do their work. Incidentally, we are lucky they have not walked away and left the produce rotting in the fields, as so many of their kind have elected to do rather than submit to the landowners' impossible demands when the yield is already so poor. Every time the beys increase taxes, the landowners take more from the fellahin so that their own revenue will not decrease even

25

though the fellahin must then work even longer hours just to have enough to survive."

Arun and Qilij exchanged a glance, their eyes returning to Maxim as he continued.

"I'm not complaining about my job, Father," Maxim said quickly, having observed the look that had passed between his father and brother.

"I know that," Qilij broke in reassuringly.

"It's just that your mamluks are quite a bit older than I am. A couple of them seem old enough to retire," Maxim continued. "The mamluks my age with whom I trained are attached to other households and spend their time with each other now that the period of training is over. Were any of them to seek me out it's very likely the others in the unit would perceive them as disloyal," Maxim said.

Qilij looked thoughtfully at Maxim.

"I think you need a different kind of challenge," Qilij said at last, "and what Arun just said gave me an idea. The Ottomans have never stopped mamluks from recruiting new slaves to train as soldiers. Why not purchase your own boys and turn them into the kind of soldier that you admire. You can train them yourself at my facility and when their training is complete you will have your own unit of soldiers endowed with the same passion for excellence that exists in you, and best of all, they will be completely loyal to you.

"By the time you have finished training them, your unit can take over the job of patrolling the land from my mamluks. Undoubtedly many of my men will be quite happy to retire by then. Since you will have charge of them it will be something meaningful to keep you busy while you wait for a war to come along. What do you think of that idea?"

"It is a wonderful idea, Father." Maxim's eyes glowed with excitement at this challenge. But then his face fell. "I don't know if I can afford to purchase any slaves though. I have been putting some money aside from my salary, but as yet my savings are meagre," he admitted ruefully.

"I can help you with that," Qilij offered. "I will lend you the money. Ten boys would be a good start, I think. There is an old barracks building near the stables that is no

26

longer used since I released several of my mamluks to seek other benefactors when I retired. It can easily be refurbished for your trainees. Separate quarters will have to be constructed close by for you as they will be young and you will need to keep an eye on them at all times. There is enough room in the stables for their horses. Think of the loan as my investment in your future, and in my own peace of mind since I will no longer have to look at your gloomy face over dinner," he ended.

Maxim was not bothered by his father's last remark. He and Arun knew this was simply how Qilij hid his immense love for his sons. He got up impulsively, walked over to his father and threw his arms around him.

"Enough! Let go of me before you crush my poor bones with your muscles!" Qilij said gruffly, making Arun laugh.

9

Two days later Maxim went to the slave market to look over the young boys who were being offered for sale. He inspected them carefully, silently wondering whether or not this one or that one would be easily seduced by vice. All the same, his task was difficult, since all imported slaves started out in the same way: as young barbarians from the Russian steppes, where life was hard and luxury non-existent. Yet, once they arrived in Egypt, many of them had ended up giving themselves over to decadence.

Maxim thought that he was probably in his twenties—the circumstances of his early life made this only his best guess—but the sight of these potential recruits made him feel much older. They appeared to be almost prepubescent; something he supposed was likely more attributable to living below subsistence levels for all of their short lives than to their actual ages. He reminisced that he had probably looked the same to Qilij that first day when fate had altered his destiny: near starvation, thin, uncared for. At best, just like him, they would have only a vague idea of how old they really were. Where he and they came from birthdays were not remembered, far less celebrated.

Some of the faces looking back at him were blank, eyes dulled from hunger and the absence of expectation. Others wore ingratiating smiles. No doubt the traders who had bought them from their parents had warned them that the most pleasing boys were usually picked first. And then there were those who kept their eyes fixed on some distant point and did not smile. Perversely, Maxim chose boys from this last group. Something about them reminded him of himself.

Centuries earlier, before the Ottomans conquered Egypt, the training of mamluks used to last six years, but as time progressed and coffers shrank in the face of social unrest and the consequent economic instability, training periods had grown considerably shorter, sometimes to as little as eighteen months. Despite that, Maxim decided that four years training would be the absolute minimum for his mamluks.

Maxim proved to be a tireless and demanding teacher. He drove his trainees to the limits of their endurance and then pushed them to dig deeper within themselves to go further. His hard work was rewarded. By the end of the four years each of his recruits had become expert in all forms of weaponry. They learned to perform military manoeuvres on horseback individually and as part of a team—how to enter a fight, how to draw back, change direction, all the while maintaining awareness of their own and their comrades' positions on the battlefield. To round out their education they were taught how to care for their horses. All had completed their religious education and had become Muslims.

But throughout the gruelling years of training his mamluks, Maxim never lost sight of what he had set out to do: create a unit that would set a new standard for soldierhood by distinguishing itself not only on the battlefield but away from it as well. Consequently, he required his mamluks to take one final step: to vow to him personally, as their benefactor, to maintain publicly and privately the traditional values of the earliest mamluks, which included strict discipline and the wearing of formal dress at all times and abstaining from sexual congress.

They took their vows gladly for they were grateful to have been chosen at all. For a young slave boy, being trained as a mamluk was a sure and certain road to fame and fortune with no one to hold them back but themselves, and just by being selected they had taken the first step on that road. Such was their gratitude that henceforth, if called upon, every single one would gladly fall on his sword for Maxim

Once their training was complete they proceeded to carry out their duties, making the rounds of Qilij's land each week to ensure no hostile faction had attempted a takeover. On other days they spent their time on drills and mock skirmishes with other mamluk units to maintain their fighting skills. Their bearing, immaculate costumes and general air of military readiness set them completely apart from their more relaxed comrades at arms, and Maxim noticed with some satisfaction that a few among the latter were now trying to emulate his mamluks.

The efficient Cairo grapevine quickly brought Maxim to the attention of Murad and Ibrahim Bey, who lost no time in making overtures of friendship, and Maxim began to receive invitations to social events that included that select group of beys, influential mamluks and wealthy Egyptians who formed the Cairo elite. Finally, two summers ago while Murad Bey was at his palace near the pyramids of Gizeh, Ibrahim Bey summoned Maxim to his palace in Ezbekiya.

When the courier arrived with the summons Maxim was at the stables grooming his horse and it was handed to Arun who happened to be in the courtyard, taking a break from his accounts. He took it immediately to Maxim, who opened and read it. Observing that Maxim's face had paled somewhat, Arun took it from his hand and perused it.

"We must seek our father's counsel immediately," Arun said. He waited while Maxim hastily finished brushing down his horse and put away his grooming paraphernalia. Together they rode quickly back to the house where Arun ordered a passing servant to find his master, beg his forgiveness for disturbing him and say that his sons wished to discuss with him a matter of some urgency and would await his pleasure in the mandara.

Qilij arrived in less than five minutes, his face betraying anxiety. It was the first time either of his sons had ever disturbed him in the middle of the day.

"Do not be anxious, Father," Maxim said, as they both went to him and embraced him in turn before leading him to the divan.

"Well, what is it?" Qilij demanded, anxiety making him sound testy.

"Ibrahim Bey has summoned me to attend him at his palace," Maxim said simply, passing the summons to his father.

Qilij read it swiftly and laid it aside.

"I have been expecting this for some time," he said. His failing health made it unlikely that he would ever be called into active duty again, but he was still a wily old soldier

30

who had cut his teeth on military political strategy. There was no doubt at all in his mind what Ibrahim Bey intended.

"More and more Ibrahim has taken charge of the administrative functions of governorship and it seems Murad is happy to leave them to him. No doubt Murad believes he is above such bureaucratic chores. He is conceited and fancies himself to be an intellectual socialite. He surrounds himself with the ulama, learned men whom he admires, and with musicians and singers. He is unkind to all except his mamluks and his retainers, and were he not in need of their protection no doubt he would show his disregard for them as well. But while Murad luxuriates in his palace Ibrahim is building his military power base. He is already sixty years old, twenty years older than Murad, and this fact will not have escaped his men. He may be afraid they will desert him and go to Murad. He likely believes that with you on his side, some of them will be tempted to stay, since many now speak of you with admiration. And it is precisely for this reason that he will perceive you as an eventual threat to him. But for now, having you on his side will allow him to sleep a little more easily at night. I am certain he will grant you the title of amir and ask you to pledge your loyalty to him. You should be careful how you respond."

"I do not see how I can refuse, Father," Maxim said.

"Nor do I. Besides which, it would be most unwise to do so. Ibrahim would interpret your refusal as an insult and he is known to revenge himself on anyone who dares to slight him."

"Then I am in the position of appearing to choose sides, am I not?"

"Not necessarily. For the moment at least, the two are acting as one and share the power equally. It is a measure of Ibrahim's uncertainty that he makes this move and forces you to his side. But I am sure that Murad's retainers keep him informed, especially on matters such as these, so be very careful of what you say and do."

"I have trained mamluks who obey my orders implicitly and others who wish to join them. How long will it be before Murad begins to believe that it is I, not Ibrahim, who may one day become his biggest threat?"

"I am sure that he will indeed reflect on that. I am only surprised that his retainers did not advise him to recruit you himself, if only so that he could keep a closer eye on you. Perhaps Baltaa whom I understand has been trying to ingratiate himself, counselled him to wait because he may perceive you as a future rival."

"You may be right, Father. Baltaa would keep me away from the centre of power if he could, since he dislikes me," Maxim said thoughtfully.

"He fears you and is jealous of you because you are a born leader of men, which is a quality that he himself does not possess in abundance," Qilij replied. "Be careful of him, but he will do nothing while you are under Ibrahim's protection. If one or the other makes a bid for complete control once again then I would not turn my back on him for an instant."

"Your advice is well taken, my father."

"Go in Allah's hands, my son."

After taking leave of their father who disappeared down the corridor Maxim and Arun walked away together in the opposite direction.

"My appointment is in one hour's time and it will take me half an hour to get there, since Ibrahim's palace is in the centre of town," Maxim said. "So I should probably get changed into something more appropriate, assuming that father is right and that Ibrahim does not intend to throw me into prison for being such an upstart."

"In which case you would be slightly overdressed," Arun replied and they both chuckled. "Were that his intention you can be sure he would not have forewarned you and wasted official paper to do so," Arun continued, laughing. "No," he concluded, "I don't think Ibrahim is the one whom you should be wary of."

"You are speaking of Baltaa," Maxim said. "What harm can he do to me, especially if I am under Ibrahim's protection?"

"I agree that he is unlikely to strike openly but if the opportunity presents itself he will use it. He will be unable to help himself. I believe that your destinies are somehow intertwined. You know what the mystics say."

"What do they say?" Maxim asked lightly, his voice betraying his innate scepticism of illogical beliefs.

"That love at first sight, or hate at first sight, are two souls recognizing each other from a previous life. They have unfinished business."

"Well, I'm certain I've never been in love with him, in this or any other life," Maxim declared jokingly, "so it appears that he and I are unlikely to arrive at a happy ending. Will you feel better if I promise to stay out of his way?"

"Yes, I would. But if that doesn't work, let him know I'm coming after him." Each was silent for few moments, as though trying to come to grips with the incongruous imagery of a sword-wielding Arun pursuing Baltaa. Then, simultaneously, the two young men gave way to howls of laughter that echoed down the corridor.

During the interview, Ibrahim's demeanour held no hint of vulnerability. He was extremely business-like. He would promote Maxim to the rank of amir and grant him a small tax farm in a village in the delta from which he would derive enough income to support himself and his ten mamluks after paying the taxes. He spoke plainly about what he expected from Maxim in return: complete loyalty and service from him and his ten mamluks. As he spoke of this, Ibrahim's eyes were riveted to Maxim's, as though trying to read into his soul. At that moment, Maxim knew that Qilij had spoken the truth. If he ever betrayed Ibrahim, his life would be worth less than two dirhems.

Maxim was aware of how fortunate he was to have received such an honour. Graciously, he expressed his gratitude to Ibrahim for his generous gift, assured him of his fidelity and left. The interview had lasted just forty-five minutes.

His ten mamluks who had waited outside the palace followed him to the al-Kvareli house where his father was waiting in the mandara to learn the outcome of the interview. Turkish coffee was brought and they celebrated his promotion together with Arun, who had hastily arrived. Maxim's throat was parched and he confided to them his opinion that Ibrahim surely deserved his reputation for being an old skinflint, since he hadn't even offered him so much as a cup of coffee during the interview.

10

1796

The Turkish viceroy was hosting an informal reception at the Citadel. It was a weekly event to which he invited amirs and other influential members of Egyptian society. Maxim was now one of the regular invitees and was attending today's event. It was one of the ways the viceroy kept himself informed since he was not much more than a figurehead. Everyone knew that the real power in Egypt was wielded by Murad and Ibrahim Bey. They and other important amirs had long since ceased to attend this informal event. Instead, they remained at the luxurious palaces they had built for themselves in and around Cairo and conducted their business from there.

About thirty people were already assembled when Maxim entered the reception room. After greeting one or two of the other regulars like himself, he moved further into the room and stood uncertainly as his eyes fell on Baltaa, who was conversing with a small group of people. Since his promotion Maxim had attended this function every week and until today, had not run into Baltaa. Briefly, he wondered what had motivated Baltaa to put in an appearance today. Was he simply making it his business as one of Murad's retainers to keep abreast of what the viceroy was up to? It was known that to weaken Murad's and Ibrahim's joint hold on power the viceroy worked behind the scenes to foment unrest among the leading amirs so that they became bitterly divided. The strategy worked: it had even resulted in some amirs being banished from Egypt for periods of time.

Seeing Baltaa, Maxim almost regretted having come, but nothing could be done about it now. Baltaa had spotted him and was already moving towards him. Much as Maxim would have wished it, there was no way to avoid the man.

"So, my young friend," Baltaa said as he arrived at Maxim's side, ""I must congratulate you on your appointment. I fancy this is only the beginning for you. It will not be long before you are promoted to an even higher rank."

"It was indeed a great honour to be promoted to the rank of amir, and had the appointment come from Murad Bey, I would have been equally honoured. As for any future promotion, the timing of that cannot be my decision. My only wish is to serve well, and if I am ever deemed worthy of further promotion, I pray that I will have acquired the necessary wisdom and experience to justify any confidence that is shown in me."

"Spoken like a true diplomat," Baltaa said. "I, for one, have no doubt that we will soon be hearing great things of you." His voice held not the slightest trace of irony, but Maxim sensed the insincerity that lay behind his words of admiration.

"I am flattered by your confidence in me," he said stiffly. "I will do everything in my power not to disappoint you." The sarcasm in his tone was unmistakable.

Baltaa flushed, seeming at a loss for words. Then he inclined his head in a cold little gesture that lay somewhere between a bow and a nod of dismissal and walked away.

Maxim stood irresolute for a brief moment. Already he regretted the impetuousness that had caused him to respond so aggressively to the hypocrisy he sensed underlying Baltaa's words. Among other things, Qilij had counselled him never to be the first to show his hand, and it seemed he was in danger of forgetting the many lessons he had learned from his father. He had allowed Baltaa to draw him out and had responded like an unsophisticated, guileless schoolboy, thrown away any future benefit he might have gained from lulling Baltaa into a false sense of security by acting the role of the ingénue. He could hardly have done worse if he had called Baltaa a hypocrite to his face. From now on, whenever they encountered each other, he knew they would be superficially civil but acutely aware of the mutual dislike that lay just below the surface, coiled for a pre-emptive strike.

Perhaps he should have played the game, but to what end? Even as a child, he had sensed enmity in Baltaa, something deep and instinctive that would never be reasoned away. Maxim suddenly remembered Arun's theory that love at first sight or hate at first sight was two souls recognizing each other from a previous life. Perhaps he and Baltaa did have unfinished business to attend to, their mutual dislike seemed so instinctive. As Maxim moved forward into the room his lips were curved in a slightly sardonic smile.

Since that encounter, he had run into Baltaa from time to time. Apart from a curt bow of acknowledgement, they more or less ignored each other. It would have been normal for them to do so even if this personal antipathy had not existed. He had pledged loyalty to Ibrahim while Baltaa owed his allegiance to Murad. When hostilities erupted between those two yet again—as it had so often in the past—he and Baltaa would not just be fighting for their respective leaders: they would have a personal score to settle.

11

January 1798

Two years had passed since Maxim and his mamluks had entered into Ibrahim's service. Maxim had become adept at the game, had learned how to avoid situations that might cast suspicion on his loyalty to Ibrahim. At the same time, he was careful to neutralize his responses to overtures from Murad's supporters, so that they went away satisfied that while he had been forced to pledge allegiance to Ibrahim, he esteemed Murad equally as a soldier.

Nevertheless, the internal politics that consumed his days had grown wearisome, and lately, he was conscious of a growing feeling of ennui, although boredom might have been too simple a word to describe what ailed him. It was more than that. He felt vaguely that it had something to do with the fact that the century was drawing to a close, or perhaps it was a feeling of having been betrayed by time: of not having accomplished enough but yet exhausted by the struggle and approaching thirty, already too old to face the prospect of what seemed like another hundred years of waiting for a war that never showed up. It was becoming increasingly difficult to keep up morale in his unit.

In the early days, when his mamluks had at last become a cohesive military unit, it had given him a certain thrill to ride through the city, conscious of the admiration of soldiers and citizenry alike. That thrill had long since evaporated, but Maxim and his mamluks still continued the practice of riding in military formation through the streets of Cairo every now and then. It broke the monotony but he knew that the cure for his imprecise longings would not be found in the alleyways of Cairo.

Today, he was going into the city to the weapons-maker to purchase a new sword which he would take to the

38

engraver to have his initials engraved in the handle. He emerged from his quarters and went out into the courtyard where his unit waited for him, mounted on their horses. The groom had brought his horse around and he handed the reins to Maxim who swung himself into the saddle and immediately urged his horse forward. His unit fell into place behind him and they left the compound, keeping the horses to a sedate walk. As they emerged into the street Maxim breathed in and exhaled deeply, as though trying to expel whatever it was that had lodged itself inside him, feeding off his energy, leaving in its place an exhausting listlessness.

It was a fine morning, a trace of coolness from the preceding night still hanging in the air. In an hour or two, the sun would reach its zenith, burning off the freshness and leaving the air redolent with the combined odour of camel and donkey droppings, leather, perfume, dyes and coffee that was the unique smell of Cairo. Already, Maxim could discern the faint buzz emanating from the city's heart, where soldiers, merchants, and veiled housewives swathed in black rubbed shoulders with strangers of every nationality in its narrow streets. Turn-of-the-century Cairo had overtaken Alexandria as the main destination and departure point for the numerous caravans, ships and barges that plied back and forth from deep within Africa to as far away as India, buying and selling wheat and barley, spices, coffee, expensive slaves and other exotic goods of every description at ports of call and villages along the Nile and across the desert, from the Red Sea to the Indian Ocean and back.

The day had only just begun but already the city was throbbing with an energy that seemed all its own, as though it had spent the night recharging itself to prepare for the onslaught of the crowds which now surged through its streets in pursuit of mundane matters. Here and there, outside the shops and inside the coffee houses, small groups of men were gathering for the important business of discussing and dissecting the previous day's events. Within these groups, one man would usually be holding forth authoritatively while his companions listened closely, nodding their heads this way or that way, depending on

whether they agreed with him or not. Once he had
orchestrated his thesis to its final triumphant conclusion—
and by now his own eloquence would have brought him to
his feet—the listeners would break out into a hubbub of
disclaimers or corollaries, drowning out all possibility of
conversation by others in the vicinity until such time that
one or the other, by dint of forcefulness, volume or
persistence, managed to gain the floor and reduce his
companions to a temporary silence.

Now and again, in the brief lulls, other voices could be
heard, words and phrases in Italian, Nubian, French,
Greek and Hebrew, tossed upon the sea of Arabic like
weightless bits and pieces of cotton, floating briefly on the
surface before being sucked under the next wave. In the
meantime, the wives hurried through the market buying,
after careful inspection, fruit, chickens and vegetables for
the meals they would later prepare to sustain their
husbands in this arduous responsibility.

As they approached the city centre Maxim, riding at the
head of his mamluks, could feel his spirits lifting as though
the surging life force all around him had been absorbed
into his veins through some kind of osmosis, temporarily
displacing the lethargy that seemed to have taken up
residence there.

As usual, the soldiers rode two abreast, breaking rank
only occasionally to navigate around a stationary or
recalcitrant donkey or camel that was blocking half the
width of the narrow street, displaying complete indifference
to the shrill imprecations of its owner who called
repeatedly upon Allah to bear witness to the unfortunate
fate that had endowed him with this stubborn, vexatious
animal.

The residents of Cairo thrived on spectacle, and the
sight of Maxim's unit in full mamluk regalia never failed to
excite the crowd who, awed and respectful, pressed against
the walls of the shops to allow them passage.

Once at the weapons-maker, Maxim took his time
selecting the perfect sword, thrusting and parrying in the
air, turning different ones this way and that till he
discovered the one whose handle felt exactly right in his
hand. By the time they arrived at the engraver's shop

which was located on a different street, almost two hours had elapsed. Maxim dismounted and leaving his horse and unit waiting in the street, pushed open the door and walked in. After he explained to the engraver exactly what he wanted, he settled down to wait. It was preferable to keep an eye on the work while it was in progress, in case the engraver became carried away with his own artistry and added some unwanted flourishes to the initials.

Maxim had been waiting for about twenty minutes when the door was opened and a heavily veiled woman entered the shop. Her presence there struck him as unusual. Except for the daily marketing, women generally left business transactions to male members of the family.

Nevertheless, after one quick glance, he averted his eyes to avoid giving the impression that he was paying particular attention to her, which would have been offensive. She was so heavily veiled that he surmised she likely belonged to the household of a very wealthy Egyptian family although, surprisingly, she was unattended by any servants.

He was more than a little shocked therefore when she walked directly up to him and said in a low voice:

"Maxim, you must help me."

In his consternation at being approached so openly and directly by a woman, one who was evidently of high caste, he almost dropped the dagger that he had been absentmindedly examining. He glanced at the engraver in alarm. For a woman to address a man publicly, even behind the anonymity of the veil, was practically unheard of. The engraver had stopped working and was looking at the woman, his mouth open in astonishment. Catching Maxim's eye, he bent his head and resumed work, appearing to concentrate fully on the engraving, but Maxim knew that his ear was cocked for any clues that would allow him to guess the woman's identity.

It was not lost on Maxim that merely by speaking to him she had placed her reputation—probably her life—in great jeopardy and he could not even begin to guess what unimaginable distress could have forced her to commit such a serious moral transgression.

41

"Continue with your work," he ordered the engraver. He moved to a corner of the shop, gesturing to the woman to follow him. The shop was so small that he was uncertain whether the engraver would be completely out of earshot, but he had no other choice. Going out into the street was even more unthinkable. He faced her, so that her back was turned to the engraver.

"Who are you?" he whispered. "What do you want?"

Instead of replying, she lifted her veil so that he could see her face and swiftly let it drop again. His eyes widened in shock. Zainab! She was now the wife of Khalid who, he knew, occupied some kind of clerical position at Ibrahim's palace. They had been married some years ago and she had disappeared behind the walls of Khalid's house. There was nothing strange in that. Once married, Egyptian women rarely went out in public, except to market. The wealthier ones were accompanied by servants or slaves to carry their purchases, as well as to keep a close eye on them and report back to the master if anything unusual occurred.

But this was no contented housewife standing in front of him. Her face was badly bruised on the left side, along the jawline, and her upper lip was swollen. She seemed completely changed. He barely recognized the child he used to know: the little girl who had laughed at him and Arun and thrown little stones at them out of pique when they refused to let her tag along behind them.

One day she had disappeared abruptly behind the veil, and Maxim had learned—in that mysterious way that young boys learn without being actually taught—that when a young girl was veiled, it meant she had become fertile, a woman, and must be prepared for marriage. Now the laughter was gone, and the look in her eyes was of such deep despair that he doubted anything could ever bring it back. In spite of all the years that he had been trained in Islamic tradition, Maxim almost reached out to touch her, but stopped instinctively.

"Khalid?" His voice was so low it was almost inaudible. She nodded, not looking up.

"Why do you not report him to the authorities?"

"I am too ashamed to show my face. He will say that I have been unfaithful and everyone will believe him."

"Why does he do this?"

"Because I do not love him," she said simply. She raised her eyes and the expression in them was almost a physical blow to Maxim. Years of celibacy had ill prepared him for the force of their bewitchingly sad and luminous appeal. He had never before been in such close proximity to a woman, seeing her face, looking into her eyes, reading unspoken messages there that her soul was translating from her hands, her lips, her body and her heart, from all the hidden places he could not see. The moment was as intensely personal as if she had stood naked before him. He felt the warmth in his face and he knew that it must have turned scarlet. She lowered her eyes and they stood there uncertainly, in the gloomy corner of the shop where the shade of the engraver's lamp cast a curving shadow.

"You wish to leave his house?" His heart was pounding, not just from the strange new emotions that had taken hold of him, but from the enormity of what he was about to propose. She nodded.

"You can never go back," he warned. She nodded again.

"Then I will ask my father tonight to take you into his house. Go to the market as usual tomorrow. If my father gives his permission, a messenger will bring you word from me. Get rid of your servant and go quickly to my father's house. You know where it is. It is not too far from here. Someone will let you in and you will be safe. Khalid will not dare to search for you there, even if he suspects where you are. Do you understand?" He paused, and she nodded again affirmatively.

"Then go now," he said."Quickly. We must not be seen together."

He waited till she had slipped out, using the few moments to collect his thoughts, hoping that the flush on his face was subsiding. Then he moved back to the counter, where the engraver was still working away meticulously.

"Are you almost through?" he asked. He thought his voice sounded quite normal.

"Just a few more minutes." He didn't look up at Maxim as he spoke, and Maxim knew that he was embarrassed to meet his eyes.

Finally, the work was done and Maxim paid him, laying the money down on the counter. He added an extra dinar for baksheesh. For a job like this, it was an extraordinarily generous tip. He walked out of the store, carrying his new sword.

12

Later that evening Maxim visited his father, hoping to see him before he retired to the harem. Arun was there and the three of them ate their evening meal together. After the servants had served them coffee and retired from the room, Maxim walked over to the divan and sat at his father's feet, exactly as he used to do when he was a boy.

"I have a favour to ask of you, Father," he said.

Qilij smiled. "If you allow your troubles to be written all over your face as they were tonight, your career as a soldier will be extremely short," he said. "I knew from the moment you walked into the room that your visit had a serious purpose."

Maxim blushed. "I apologize if I have been dull company, Father. If I seem anxious, it is simply because I fear that what I have to ask may place you in a very awkward position."

Qilij regarded him steadily. "Speak," he said.

"The woman Zainab, who is the wife of Khalid, one of Ibrahim's clerks, followed me into the engraver's shop today and implored my help. She wishes to leave the house of Khalid and I have promised to ask if you will take her into your house."

On hearing this, Arun got up from the divan where he was seated and walked across the room to sit on the floor opposite to Maxim. Qilij did not reply at first. He seemed to be deep in thought and Maxim feared he had made his father very angry.

"I am truly sorry, Father," he said, looking distressed. "But when the woman cried out to me for help, I could not refuse her."

"This action does strike me as extremely strange, and more so for one who is now an amir. You may be accused of committing adultery with this woman, and she herself

45

may suffer greatly for her sins against Islam, which teaches that a husband may indeed chastise his wife if she has committed wrongdoing."

"But she has done no wrong, Father," Maxim said, his voice quieter now. "Except that she is unable to love her husband, for which he beats her, and her face is disfigured from the beatings."

Qilij raised his eyebrows, causing Maxim to wonder which had surprised him more—the fact that she had revealed her face to a man, or the fact that the beating had marred her face.

"Are there children from the marriage?" he asked, addressing Arun, whom he knew to be more informed than either himself or Maxim about the ordinary lives of the townspeople.

"No, Father. I have heard tell that Khalid has been most disappointed about Zainab's failure to provide him with sons."

"Then why does he not simply divorce her and take a new wife who is fertile."

"I have known Khalid practically since infancy," Arun said."He cannot bear to part with what he considers his rightful property. He is selfish, like a dog that keeps his bone hidden even though it may be dried up and of no use to him."

"Did you not say at the time of the marriage that he paid an extremely high bride price?" Maxim asked.

"So he did. Zainab was unwilling to marry him and refused him for three years. She has been indulged by her father, who allowed her to converse with foreign women and it gave her ideas not suited to our way of life. He did not force her to accept Khalid as her husband until the bride price he offered was so high that no sensible man could have refused. I am told that he offered money, jewellery and property that will take him the remainder of his life to pay for. By the time she agreed to marry him, Khalid was a laughingstock among the townspeople, but he would have no other for his wife. But I fear that he still feels resentment towards her."

"If he displays cruelty towards her, why does she not simply seek the permission of the courts to divorce him?"

"She will have to prove it by showing her face to the judges, Father, and she is ashamed to let them see her in that condition. Besides, he has threatened to say she is an unfaithful wife and she fears that they will believe him."

Qilij sipped his coffee and seemed to fall into deep thought, while Maxim and Arun regarded him and each other in silence, awaiting his decision. Then:

"Did anyone observe you in conversation with her?"

"Only the engraver, but naturally, she did not reveal her face to him. He heard her speak, but I do not see how he can be certain of her identity. In any case, I paid him handsomely to encourage him to remain uncertain."

"He will remain uncertain only so long as it is in his best interest to do so," Arun commented.

"What is it that you feel for this woman?" Qilij demanded.

"I pitied her situation," Maxim replied. "Other than that, I cannot say, because I do not know. I do not want her, or anyone else, for a wife, if that is what you mean."

"I would not want to see you ruin your career with such an unsuitable alliance. In any case, she must now live out her days in seclusion, since she is leaving her husband's house without the court's permission and will therefore be unsafe from him if he should find her. I take it you have made some arrangement to contact her again?"

"I told her to come to the market tomorrow and a messenger would find her. If you give your permission, she will come here directly."

"Good. Then I will send one of my women. She will find her easily I am sure, and I will also send Qualub, my most trusted personal mamluk, to ensure that she is not followed by a spying servant on her way here. She will be provided with private quarters under my roof until I can decide what is to be done with her. You, Maxim," he continued, "must ensure that you pass the entire day with your unit so that they can vouch for your whereabouts if necessary. If perchance anyone should dare to point a finger at you in connection with her disappearance, it must be dismissed as pure speculation."

"Thank you, Father," Maxim said simply.

"Go now, both of you," Qilij said. He stood up and embraced them. "You young people wear me out." His eyes held a little twinkle.

Maxim lay awake that night staring into the darkness for a long time, thinking about the possible repercussions of his instinctive reaction to Zainab's plea for help. Why was he taking such a risk, providing sanctuary for a woman who wished to leave her husband? Even if he had the answer, would he have acted differently? It was pointless to speculate on that now. The die was cast and it was too late to change the course of events he had set in motion.

Should the matter ever become public, his actions would certainly be considered unusual by those who were in a position to judge him. Mamluks rarely concerned themselves with the personal lives of Egyptians. The wealthy ones took the women into their harems, and as a matter of course, fathered children who were raised in the harem. There were exceptions. Some mamluks had been known to become very attached to their women and children. His father, for example. Deep inside he must have known his father would not refuse to help him; otherwise he would not have asked.

Qilij was one of those rare exceptions, a mamluk who was guided by his own consciousness of right and wrong. His mamluks, his women and his children had been the beneficiaries of the fairness and generosity that had resulted. Was he, Maxim, about to follow in his father's footsteps? But his father was old now, retired, and free to indulge himself as he pleased. Maxim's career was just beginning. His actions might be perceived as a sign of weakness, a lowering of caste.

All he knew was that on seeing Zainab's bruised face he had instinctively wanted to punish Khalid and the desire to make him suffer had not yet passed from him. Was that why he had agreed to help her? To get even with Khalid?

What went on in Egyptian families behind closed doors was a private matter and meddling from an outsider, he knew, was completely unacceptable. The wealthier families had considerable influence in the city and were treated with respect, at least on the surface. The de facto government depended on them to carry out the bureaucratic functions because mamluks were better at wielding swords, not pens. The Egyptians kept things running smoothly. If they should learn of his interference in the private life of one of their own, they might be alarmed at the idea that he was somehow setting a precedent and complain to their superiors, who were also his superiors. It would surely hurt his career to have them annoyed with him for disrupting the smooth machinery of government.

But it was difficult to focus on these consequences when his mind insisted on returning to the feelings that Zainab had aroused in him. Her face suddenly swam before his eyes and his heart beat faster as he recalled the look he had seen in the dark wells of her eyes. He had never gazed so openly on a woman's face before. He closed his eyes, breathing deeply and evenly, fighting to restore his equilibrium so that sleep could prevail.

13

The following day he was tense, edgy, half-expecting a messenger at any moment who would have been sent, either by Arun or his father—or heaven forbid, by Zainab herself—telling him that she couldn't go through with it or that she had been prevented from doing so by Khalid or one of his spies. Mindful of his father's advice, he stayed with his unit, passing the time playing chess and polo, and practising on the training field with them, shooting arrows at a target while in full gallop.

As the sun travelled across the sky from east to west, he found himself mentally picturing each phase of the scenario that was unfolding on the outside with the progression of the day. Zainab discreetly hurrying from the market accompanied by the woman from his father's harem. She would be keeping her head down. Although veiled up to the eyes she would still be deathly afraid of being recognized. What fear she must feel! What if Khalid's suspicions had somehow been aroused and she was being spied on? But no. His father's most trusted mamluk would find a way to divert anyone who might be following her.

On leaving the busy market area, although indistinguishable from scores of other women swathed in black, she would be feeling more exposed, more terrified. He saw her arrive at the house and the gate being immediately opened. She would stumble at the entrance, almost fainting with terror and dread, because the step she was about to take would be irrevocable. She would be led to the private quarters that had been prepared for her, given something to calm her nerves and then left alone for the time being.

At dusk, he pictured the scene at Khalid's house when he returned home and the servants reported that she was missing. It would be near dark then, the shops and houses would already have their shutters drawn and doors locked.

The gates would be barred against all intruders, as Cairo shut itself up against the dangers of the night. Khalid would nevertheless send his servants to search the streets. The market area would be completely deserted. They would be almost afraid to go back and report to him that they had found nothing, had seen nothing unusual.

His mind raced ahead to the following day. Khalid would begin making discreet enquiries so as to avoid suspicion and gossip, because his honour would be at stake. He would know that she could not have gone far without help. Then his mind would begin to revolve maddeningly, identifying and eliminating, until there remained at the very centre of the nucleus the few pitiful choices that would have been open to her.

Maxim recalled Arun's words: "You must have a death wish," he had said last night when Qilij was out of earshot. "Khalid will kill you if he finds out you have played a part in this, even if it should cost him his own life." If Zainab did go to his father's house and his part in her disappearance from her husband's house became known, Khalid would certainly feel obliged to revenge his honour by killing him, mamluk or not. And no Egyptian court would condemn him for what they felt he had a right, even a duty, to do.

Nevertheless, Maxim's interaction with Zainab and the prospect of a challenge from Khalid were affecting him like a shot of adrenalin in his veins, heightening his mental and emotional awareness. Maxim reflected that if he did indeed have a death wish, its effect on him was the complete opposite, because he suddenly realized that he hadn't felt so alive in months.

14

The following morning, as soon as he awoke, Maxim's first thought was of Zainab, who should have been safely installed in his father's house by now. He would not learn the details until the next day when he would go into the city to meet Arun at a coffee house. They had decided that he should not return to his father's house just yet. Since moving out to the barracks his duties kept him occupied and he had gotten into the habit of visiting his father once each week. Since he had visited him only two nights ago, returning there too soon might seem a little unusual to anyone who might be keeping an eye on him. It was imperative that he not change his routine.

This morning, Murad Bey was hosting a service to celebrate the restoration of the 'Amr Ibn al-'As mosque, the first mosque to be built in Cairo. Originally completed in 642 the mosque was now well over a thousand years old. It had been demolished and rebuilt several times since it was first erected and had grown larger and more resplendent with each modification. Since the last repair some of the columns had collapsed and Murad had had it demolished and rebuilt.

Murad was known to be haughty and arrogant and recently had become somewhat reclusive. Foregoing even the company of his amirs he now secluded himself at his Giza palace with only his friends and retainers for company. When the invitation to the service arrived Maxim was flattered to have been included. He had no doubt that the invitees would include everyone of importance in Cairo and that they would all attend. Invitations from Murad were rare and none would pass up the chance to meet not only with him—he was, after all, one of the joint governors —but with each other. It was an opportunity no one would want to miss and Maxim fully intended to be there.

By ten-thirty the elite of Cairo were assembled in the prayer hall: the amirs, the judges, the religious leaders, influential Egyptians, foreign ambassadors. The brilliant robes of the mamluks, in exquisite silks and satins of every hue, dominated the hall in a kaleidoscope of shifting colour that was reflected like myriad points of multicoloured lights in the jewelled turbans adorning their heads. Maxim himself was magnificently attired in a turquoise silk robe and soft white velvet boots. On his head he wore a white silk turban, in the centre of which a fiery emerald sparkled.

As the service proceeded, the ritual movements of the worshippers as they repeatedly prostrated themselves and returned to upright positions created an impression of a restless sea of colour in which the more sober costumes of the judges and the religious leaders opened up tiny oases of tranquillity. The movement, the bright colours, the long flowing robes and sparkling jewels combined to lend an air of beauty and festiveness to the occasion that would otherwise have been lacking.

Once the service was over the guests withdrew to an adjoining area for light refreshments and the customary presentation of gifts of appreciation to the more distinguished guests. After the presentation the guests seized the moment to mingle before leaving and Maxim retreated to the sidelines from where he could observe and enjoy the spectacle.

Maxim knew that the cultured elegance displayed before him masked a hard and determined purpose and he observed with amusement how the invitees immediately turned their attention to the politics which for them was almost literally the breath of life. Certain beys fawned around Ibrahim and Murad Bey, the joint governors, who were themselves busy courting the foreign ambassadors, conscious of the necessity to cement relations with allies whose assistance might have to be sought, either to support a coup, or to provide a haven in the event that it failed.

The merchants, like their counterparts throughout history, fawned on all equally, from the administrators who might be persuaded to revisit the issue of their tax arrears, to the judges who would finally decide the inevitable court case, through to the ambassadors of those countries where they hoped to find bigger markets for their merchandise.

Murad Bey was holding court in the middle of the room, displaying his talents as host to the crowd which now pressed around him. They appeared intent on taking full advantage of this opportunity to hear his views firsthand and Maxim smiled as snatches of conversation drifted past his ear, confirming his suspicions that their motivation to attend the service was firmly rooted in the here and now and had little to do with religion.

Rumours had been circulating, perhaps brought back by French merchants living in Cairo, of French and English warships chasing each other across the Mediterranean Sea and some feared a French invasion of Egypt might be imminent. After all, they had tried it once before. Murad scornfully dismissed the rumours, poking fun at the very idea of French cavalry charging across the desert, itching miserably from the unaccustomed heat, their heavy tunics drenched with sweat. Judging by the frequent bursts of laughter emitted by his audience, Murad was evidently in high spirits for a change. Nevertheless, from his vantage point on the sidelines, Maxim observed that the smiles of some of the foreign ambassadors standing together on the edge of the admiring crowd seemed a trifle forced.

"A splendid occasion, is it not?" Maxim recognized the voice of Baltaa and turned to face him, hiding his surprise. He could swear that only a few seconds ago he had caught sight of him on the other side of the room, at the elbow of Murad Bey. The man moves with such stealth, he thought, like a crocodile, crawling quietly through the long grass to pounce on his victim.

"Most splendid," Maxim replied, carefully maintaining an air of agreeable composure. After their conversation at the viceroy's reception he had resolved to never again allow Baltaa to discern his innermost thoughts. "The ordinary citizens must be extremely gratified to see how well their money has been spent," he added, referring to the citizens whose money, he knew, had been unlawfully prised out of their hands to pay for the rebuilding. Though not formally invited they had exercised their Muslim right to enter the mosque to pray.

He was conscious of Baltaa scrutinizing him, trying to determine whether he spoke tongue-in-cheek or not, and he smiled inwardly. Two can play at this game, he thought smugly.

"Yes," Baltaa replied smoothly. "As you can see they have turned out in great numbers for this occasion. The poorest peasant understands the importance of setting aside proper places where all can pray and worship without distraction."

"I am sure that they do," Maxim agreed. "And that they also understand the need to richly reward their spiritual leaders without whose guidance they would be lost. One can only hope that the happiness they must now feel at being able to show their gratitude with such generous gifts will sustain them as they go about their daily lives." Maxim was baiting Baltaa now, but his face and voice betrayed not a trace of sarcasm. In fact, he realized that he was enjoying being undetectably perverse.

"Speaking of happiness," Baltaa replied, "a misfortune has befallen one of our auditors, a fellow called Khalid, the son of our chief shop inspector. I believe you know him? It seems that his wife has disappeared and he fears some harm may have come to her."

"That is indeed a great misfortune," Maxim replied gravely, instantly on his guard. "Has a search been conducted?"

"Enquiries have been made," Baltaa replied smoothly. "But as you know, it is not possible to search every house in Cairo."

"I would not have thought that such a search would be necessary. It is hard to believe that any Egyptian family in the city would knowingly harbour the woman. Perhaps she has joined a caravan?" he suggested.

"I do not think so. As a matter of fact, one of the servants reported that she thought she saw her mistress in the company of another woman yesterday morning. She was hurrying to catch up to them when she tripped and fell, striking her head on the cobblestone. By the time she recovered, she had lost sight of them."

"The whole thing is indeed strange," Maxim said musingly.

"Yes, it is," Baltaa said, regarding Maxim closely. "And what is more strange is that the servant thought that the woman accompanying her mistress might have been someone she knew from your father's house."

"Then I will certainly ask my father the next time I visit him whether anything unusual has been brought to his attention," Maxim replied. "But, as you know, my father's health is failing and he now concerns himself very little with the world outside."

"Pray do not trouble him unnecessarily," Baltaa said smoothly. "I have advised this Khalid that we will do what we can. However, there are very few secrets among the Egyptians themselves, and sooner or later, through talk among them, I expect that some light will be shed on this mystery. Now, my young friend, I must ask you to excuse me. I think I am needed elsewhere." Before Maxim could respond, Baltaa had departed from his side.

Maxim watched his saffron robe weaving through the crowd, adding one more brilliant patch to the Jacob's coat of riotous colour decorating the room. He let his breath out unobtrusively. Up until then, he had not realized that he had been holding it. Baltaa's warning had been clear. Egyptians loved to gossip, he knew, and servants in particular engaged in a form of revengeful solidarity peculiar to the lower classes that impelled them to divulge to each other their employers' most personal secrets, thus regaining in private the sense of power denied to them in public. But his father's servants were among the most loyal, he knew, and his women were devoted to him.

When the service ended Baltaa was nowhere to be seen and Maxim wondered uneasily whether his absence had any connection with Zainab's disappearance and whether it was only a question of time before her presence in his father's house became public knowledge.

15

The morning following the service Maxim opened his eyes, relieved to find that he had, after all, gotten some sleep. Lying sleepless in the dark had somehow magnified his guilt over the difficulty in which he now realized he had placed his father, Arun, Zainab and indeed, the entire household.

He wondered whether he had not finally presented Baltaa with the opportunity he had waited for all these years. If he was disgraced, his tax farm would be withdrawn for redistribution by Ibrahim as he saw fit. If such a thing came to pass, Maxim had no doubt at all that most of it would somehow end up in Baltaa's hands, if that one continued to play his cards right. He was well-placed to do it since it was clear that Murad Bey was slowly gaining ascendancy over Ibrahim. The writing was on the wall and Maxim had even begun to think seriously about the consequences of that for his own position.

But in the meantime, there were more immediate problems to be solved, the main one being to decide whether a safer place could be found for Zainab. It was clear that Baltaa suspected his involvement in her disappearance. Khalid acting alone was not powerful enough or influential enough to commission a search of his father's house, but with Baltaa on his side, it might happen, if it suited Baltaa's plans, because Baltaa was a mamluk, one who would have some influence.

By now Maxim was fully dressed, but he remained in his quarters, pacing back and forth. Another interminable hour must pass before the coffee shops opened their doors and he could meet with Arun as they had arranged. He would be bringing him news of Zainab and perhaps together they could devise a plan. About ten minutes later he stopped stock still in the centre of the room. He couldn't very well pace for an hour, he decided. He might as well go

57

over to the barracks dining area where his unit was served their meals. At least there would be coffee and sweet rolls. He opened the door and almost barged into his servant, who was apparently about to knock.

"What is it?" he inquired curiously. Usually, the man would not intrude, but hovered outside the door in case he was needed.

"A servant brought this message from your father's house, master," he said, reaching into a concealed pocket in the folds of his tunic and withdrawing a piece of paper. He handed it to Maxim, who took it and tore it open hastily. His face went white as he read what Arun had written on it.

"Have my horse brought around at once," he barked to the surprised servant, who scuttled obediently away. A few seconds later Maxim charged out of his quarters, his sword rattling against his leg and a carbine slung over his shoulder.

Two of his mamluks were already in the courtyard waiting to assemble to accompany him to the city. "Get the others and go directly to my father's house to ensure that no one enters," he said to one. "I will join you there. Move quickly!" He gestured to the second soldier: "You, follow me!" he ordered as the groom came running up to him leading his horse. Maxim hoisted himself into the saddle and rode out of the compound.

He reached his destination in minutes: the prison where Arun's note said his father had been taken. Dismounting, he pounded imperiously on the gate until the jailer appeared, peering at him nervously through the grillwork with his one good eye.

"I am Maxim bin Kvareli," he said loudly. "My father was brought here early this morning. Where is he? Bring him to me immediately!"

"Not allowed," the jailer whined. "Prisoner need official paper to come in, official paper to go out."

Maxim brought his face up to the grillwork and glared threateningly at the jailer, who backed three feet away and seemed to be contemplating whether the gate was strong enough to withstand an assault from Maxim.

"Show me the official paper," Maxim said, his voice deadly with anger.

"Yes sir, yes sir, I have it right here." He held up a piece of paper, just out of Maxim's reach, so that he could barely read what was written on it. There seemed to be six names on the list and something about evading taxes. The authorizing signature was an unreadable scrawl, but Maxim knew that it was probably signed by Ibrahim's chief tax collector.

"Open this gate at once or I promise you will sleep with your ancestors tonight," he said menacingly to the jailer. "And if one hair of his head has been harmed, you will wish that this was indeed the last day of your miserable life."

His words seemed to galvanize the jailer, who stumbled forward, his eye watering with fright:

"At once, sir, at once sir," he repeated.

He lifted the heavy bar that secured the gate and Maxim and his mamluk charged through, pushing open the gate which swung inward, knocking over the jailer. Maxim grabbed him by the folds of his tunic and hauled him to his feet:

"Take me to my father," he commanded. Cowed, the jailer led them to the cell where Qilij had been detained separately and opened it. Maxim's face reddened with anger at the sight of his father, still in his night clothes. He must have been dragged out of bed and taken to prison. Qilij looked relieved, but seemed to be not too much the worse for wear.

"Come, Father," Maxim said. "I am taking you home."

"If your father wishes to use my horse to return to his house, I will follow on foot," his mamluk suggested as they got outside. Maxim pressed his shoulder in unspoken gratitude and as soon as his father was mounted, they set off for home, the soldier running behind.

When they arrived at the house, Maxim saw that his mamluks had taken up positions outside the gate and in the courtyard. As they walked up the steps leading to the mandara, Arun came hurrying out:

"Praise be to Allah you are safe, Father," he burst out. "And you also, Maxim. The women have been distraught with worry."

"No harm has come to me," Qilij said. "At least I was separated from the other prisoners, so that my sojourn was less unpleasant than it might have been. I am more concerned now about the nature of the charges that were laid against me, which of course were completely false."

"Do not concern yourself about that, father. I will take care of it. You must rest now. It is plain to see you are weary from your ordeal."

He turned to Arun. "Take our father upstairs where he can be made comfortable," he said to him. "Then you will accompany me to Ibrahim's residence. After I have spoken with him you may be needed to verify the accounts you submitted."

As he waited for Arun in the mandara, Zainab suddenly appeared. He knew it was her, even though her face was veiled.

"I have brought trouble to your father's house," she said. "I am certain that Khalid must suspect that I am here and that is why he has falsified your father's accounts so that he would be arrested. I see his hand in this because he has exacted revenge before in this way and boasted to me about it. If I do not return to him, Arun will be next."

"You must know what will happen if you return to him," Maxim replied. "You will be safe from him as long as you remain here. And now that he has dared to act against my family, I am determined that he shall not prevail, and I will avenge this insult to my father."

"I do not plan to go back to him," she said. "But I am afraid of what he might do. Be very careful, I beseech you. He is a dangerous man." Her eyes rested on his face in forceful appeal and he felt again that strange stirring in his breast. Before he could reply, she withdrew quietly, leaving behind a delicate scent of jasmine that hovered momentarily in the air and then it, too, was gone.

Ordering six of his mamluks to remain stationed at the house, Maxim rode to Ibrahim's palace, accompanied by the other four and Arun. Splitting the soldiers into two detachments made him feel exposed. Ten mamluks were inadequate to protect both himself and his family, he now saw, and a new ambition was suddenly born in him. He resolved to acquire more mamluks as soon as possible.

When they arrived the guards at the gate recognized him. They admitted him and he and Arun were taken straight to Ibrahim's offices where a duty officer was posted. He demanded an urgent audience with Ibrahim and was told to sit in the waiting room with Arun while his request was relayed. Finally, one of Ibrahim's personal mamluks appeared and requested that he alone follow him.

"Wait here," he said to Arun.

Ibrahim appeared to be in an expansive mood for a change.

"Good morning, Maxim," he said, indicating that he should be seated. "I am told that there is some kind of emergency? How can I help you?"

Maxim came right to the point.

"I have just returned from the prison where my father was being unjustly detained on false charges," he said, his voice indignant.

"Indeed!" Ibrahim sounded surprised. "Of what has he been accused?"

"Of tax evasion," Maxim declared bluntly. "He is charged with remitting an amount of tribute to the State that is lower than it should be, based on the income collected from his holdings. This is completely false and can be easily disproven by an examination of the records. My father's natural son who manages my father's accounts will verify the amounts submitted, which he prepared in his own hand."

"I have known your father for many years," Ibrahim said. "No doubt some clerical error has been made. I will send for my chief tax collector so that this matter can be cleared up immediately." He rang a small bell on the desk and the duty officer appeared.

"Send for the chief tax collector," he said to him. "I wish to see him at once." The duty officer nodded and shut the door again.

"I will see that the charges are quashed and that your father is returned forthwith to his house," Ibrahim said.

"I obtained my father's release and took him home before coming here," Maxim said. "His health is failing and he cannot easily endure the rigours of being dragged out of his house in the early morning hours and left in a prison cell clad only in his night clothes."

"But, I am scandalized at the treatment he has received." Ibrahim's tone was astounded. Before he could say more, there was a light knock on the door and Ibrahim's chief tax collector entered: short, plump and even though it was still fairly early in the morning, perspiring profusely. He listened while Ibrahim outlined the problem, glancing nervously from time to time at Maxim, who was glaring at him in unconcealed anger.

"I was unaware of this unfortunate occurrence," he said. "The lists are merely presented to me for authorization after the accounts have been verified by the auditors, I will go now and personally review the Kvareli accounts for this month and report my findings back to you immediately," he said. "There has never been a problem before."

"Do so," Ibrahim ordered.

He was back in ten minutes. "My humble apologies," he said, wringing his hands in distress. "There was no discrepancy in the accounts reported by Commander al-Kvareli. It is the fault of the auditor, one Khalid, who has made an error in his calculations. I have dismissed him effective immediately and he is on his way out of the palace at this very moment."

"And you will follow him for not having even questioned why an account that has been in good standing for many years is suddenly in arrears," Ibrahim said sternly. "You seemed unaware that the Kvareli name was even on the list. It appears to me that you sign documents without fully reading them, which makes you unreliable. But before you leave, prepare a letter of apology to Commander al-Kvareli, which I will sign, for the unconscionable treatment he has suffered and have it on my desk within the hour. Now go!"

As the now weeping chief tax collector stumbled out the door, Ibrahim turned to Maxim: "My dear fellow," he said, "I deeply regret this matter and trust that your father will be no worse for wear after this unfortunate experience. Please convey to him my sincere apologies. As you heard, the two who were responsible have been dismissed from their posts and a letter of apology will be sent to your father by courier this very day. Is that satisfactory?"

"Entirely," Maxim said. "I thank you for your assistance. My father will be most pleased to hear that his good name has not been jeopardized."

"Then I wish you good day," Ibrahim said, and walked him to the door.

"I will escort you back home," Maxim said to Arun when they got outside. "Khalid and the chief tax collector have both been dismissed and it is possible Khalid for one will seek to revenge himself against you personally."

As they rode through the city, at a much slower pace this time, Maxim could feel the white hot anger that had consumed him since he first received Arun's note beginning to subside.

"Let us stop and have a cup of coffee together," he suggested, as they came up to a coffee shop that was well known for its excellent brew. "Perhaps it will help to calm me, for to tell you the truth, I am still angry at the way our father was treated, incarcerated in a cell that stank of years of stale urine."

They entered the shop and sat down at a small table in the middle, gesturing to the proprietor to bring them two coffees. Two of Maxim's four mamluks dismounted from their horses and stationed themselves just outside the door, while the other two remained mounted in the street.

"How was it possible that they were able to enter the house," Maxim wanted to know.

"He was taken by surprise," Arun replied. "As you know, he strolls around the courtyard in the early morning to benefit from the fresh air and exercise. The soldiers rushed in and easily overpowered Qualub."

"Perhaps he should have kept more of his mamluks. Obviously the few he retained cannot be in two places at once. When they are out on patrol he is not adequately protected by Qualub alone even though he is retired and rarely leaves the house. I was careless. When I went into Ibrahim's service with my unit I should have realized that would be the case," Maxim added, despondent.

"Do not blame yourself," Arun told him. "Had it not been for Khalid, he would have been perfectly safe in his retirement. Is there ever any protection from such a one as that?"

The coffee was brought to the table and Maxim waited until the server had walked away before answering.

"Khalid may have had some idea of having the house searched. Did they enter the house at all?"

"No, because there would have been no reason to. They came for our father and he was right there in the courtyard."

"I take it that Zainab is safely installed in the house?" Maxim asked in a low voice.

"Yes. When she heard the commotion in the courtyard she looked through the mashrabiya and saw what was happening. After our father was taken away, she went into the harem to comfort the women, who had become hysterical."

"She has much courage, that one," Maxim said.

"She was prepared to return to Khalid's house if necessary, to ensure our father would be released from jail, but I persuaded her not to."

"That would have been foolish in the extreme," Maxim replied. "Even if he didn't kill her, she would soon be wishing that he had."

"Why is this half-caste son of a peasant allowed to sit among decent people?" said a loud voice from the door. All conversation ceased abruptly in the coffee shop and Maxim jumped to his feet, his hand already reaching for his sword. His reaction was instantaneous. He had known it would be Khalid before he even turned around to face him.

"No. No." Arun said, restraining Maxim. "I am the one he wishes to attack. Do not sully your sword with the blood of this hyena."

"I am tired of him," Maxim said bluntly, his hand still on his sword.

"I will deal with it," Arun said.

"Answer me, eunuch," Khalid taunted.

"I pity you," Arun said, rising and walking over to where Khalid was standing. "The hate that eats at you has cost you dear. Do you not see how it has destroyed your life? It has robbed you of your wife and today it has cost you your job. Why do you not cease before it ends up costing you your life?"

Khalid looked at him, his face working contortedly.

"It is you who will die!" he screamed suddenly, and drawing out a dagger that was hidden in the sleeve of his galabiyah, he moved forward with an excited little jump and plunged it into the side of Arun's neck. For one split second Maxim felt as though he were standing outside himself, watching in horror as the world erupted around him. Dreamlike, he was aware of two of his mamluks rushing through the door, followed closely by two more, of all four of them surrounding him with swords drawn, protecting him. At the same time he saw Arun stagger backward, saw blood dripping from his neck, staining his clothing. The sight galvanized Maxim and propelled him forward just in time to catch Arun in his arms as he fell to the floor. Blood was now pouring out of the wound and Maxim put his hand over it, attempting vainly to close it up and stop the flow of blood. Arun caught his hand and as his eyes met Maxim's, he gave a strangled little cough, his head fell back and his fingers released their hold on Maxim's hand.

Maxim had the impression that the world had stopped and all its sounds had melded together in a blur of white noise that was beginning in some place far away as he watched Arun's soul struggle free: the final tremor of his body as the soul paused for an instant like a newly-emerged butterfly that is loath to leave its familiar shelter, before winging its way onward through eternity. Arun was gone. With a shudder that signified the beginning of an insupportable grief, Maxim relinquished his hold on his brother's lifeless body and laid it on the floor.

And now the echo of the strange and terrible noise, coming from he knew not where, was vibrating deep within him, gathering strength as it rolled upwards and outwards, until it burst from Maxim's lips in a primeval roar of anguish and rage that was the sound of his very soul shattering. The force of his cry propelled him upward and flowed into his right arm as he drew his sword and, whirling around and swinging with all his might, he decapitated Khalid.

The head fell off and hit the floor with a dull thud, while the torso collapsed, twitching, at Arun's feet, purply red blood gushing like wet rope out of the neck and mixing with Arun's blood that was now streaming across the floor, macabre fate uniting in death two who had lived as enemies.

The sword dropped from Maxim's hand and he stood there, teetering on the edge of the yawning abyss that had suddenly opened up inside him, as though his roar of pain in its headlong rush to emerge from his body, had swept away everything in its path with the force of a volcano.

The mind shies away from acknowledging terrible events as though it possesses some preternatural instinct that to absorb such knowledge would certainly drive a human mad. So it was with Maxim, as his mind plunged into the blessed safety of nothingness. It was only later that it permitted him to recall, little by little, the frightened expressions of the proprietor and the handful of early morning customers in the coffee shop who had witnessed the double homicide that would sustain their discussions for weeks to come, and being taken from the scene by his mamluks who would later swear before the judge that Maxim had acted in self-defence.

He would, however, forever recall with painful clarity the extinguishing of the light in Qilij's eyes when the body of his first son was brought home; the lamentations of the servants and the women of the house as he and his father removed Arun's galabiyah, the crimson stains already turning brown in the hot dry air, and wrapped the body in sheets of white cloth to await the washer of the corpse; and finally, the face of Zainab, lips pressed tight, skin taut so that the bruise on her face stood out like a splotch of dark wine, her eyes echoing a perpetual scream of guilt and self-recrimination that was all the more terrible for its strange-sounding noiselessness.

16

The news spread quickly and the mourners began to fill the house and courtyard, spilling out even into the street. Arun was known and liked by the townspeople. While Maxim had been preoccupied with forming his unit of young soldiers, Arun had gone quietly about the city, attending efficiently and courteously to his father's business. The fellahin who worked the land were also arriving to pay their respects, wearing their best clothes. Arun had collected the taxes from them, but he had treated them fairly, humanely, avoiding raising taxes until it was absolutely necessary, and not at all during those terrible years of low Niles. The fellahin, resigned to lucklessness, would have very little hope that the new tax collector, whoever he might be, would exercise a similar restraint.

When the corpse washer arrived Maxim retreated with his father to the mandara, leaving the washer to the task of preparing Arun for his journey to eternity. The mandara was crowded with people, most of whom Maxim realized were strangers to him. These men, their faces grave and sorrowful, were merchants and businessmen who, after years of business transactions with Arun, carried out in a civilized fashion over cups of coffee, had become his friends. Above their murmured words of sympathy Maxim could hear the weeping of the women in the harem.

Kurjii al Saleh was there, constant at his father's side, and one or two other retired soldiers who had also become his companions over the past ten years. Baltaa arrived, paid his respects and after a civilized interval, departed. Baltaa and Qilij had grown distant, separated by philosophical differences in their regard for the fellahin who, to Baltaa, had been more or less a contemptible utility.

Glancing through the mashrabiya, Maxim could see his mamluks grouped in one corner of the courtyard with their horses and it hit him with the force of a blow to the stomach that these men were there out of simple solidarity with their benefactor. They could not possibly share his grief, and he wondered if they were even capable of understanding it. As he watched them standing there, his trained and disciplined unit waiting quietly for their next orders, his heart began to beat - wildly and painfully - because he knew himself to be suddenly and completely alone, bereft of the only true companion he had ever known.

He turned around abruptly to face the room where so many had gathered to mourn the passing of Arun. When death came to claim him, there would be no one to mourn him as he mourned Arun. Soldiers would come to pay their respects, and the official mourners would leave as soon as they had completed the agreed-upon hours. He felt cold, as though the fire of ambition that had warmed him for so many years had been suddenly extinguished, and he could almost taste the ashes. He moved to his father's side, seeking warmth in the only place where he would find it, knowing that there too, time was his enemy.

17

The following morning when the sun had risen fully he walked with Qilij behind the bier as it was borne out of the house to the mosque. As the procession wound its way through the streets, moving quickly because burial must occur as soon as possible after death, Maxim recalled the many occasions he and Arun had ridden through these very streets: two lively boys forever in a hurry to get to somewhere, sometimes taking shortcuts with their prayers to save time, because boys will be boys no matter where they live.

The funeral prayers were recited in the courtyard of the mosque with Qilij and Maxim standing next to one another behind the imam and the other mourners in rows behind them. As they confirmed aloud that Arun had indeed been one of the pious, it seemed to Maxim that truer words had never been spoken. His brother had been pure of heart and that testimony must surely be borne upwards to Allah, carried on a cloud of incense perfumed by the delicate scent of rosewater that had been sprinkled on Arun's forehead, nose, hands, feet and knees.

As they reached the cemetery outside the city walls, Maxim perceived the grave that was waiting to receive his brother and the dead heavy thing that had been his heart burst into life with a piercing throb of pain, becoming a monstrous mass that filled his chest so tightly he thought it would explode. Maxim watched, eyes almost unseeing, so great was his grief, as Arun's body, turned to Mecca, was placed in the grave which was then closed up with sand. Finally, he could no longer see Arun's body and with that, miraculously, he felt his pain easing, so that he could breathe again, force the life-sustaining air past that wounded bleeding heart so swollen and heavy with grief.

After the gifts of bread and dates had been distributed to the poor and the official mourners were paid, Maxim and

Qilij walked back to the house, willing their feet to continue taking step after reluctant step, and it seemed to Maxim that at any minute he would turn around and go back, that he could not leave Arun behind. As they entered the house Maxim heard the soft weeping of the women and tears ran down his face.

18

Maxim passed the three days of mourning secluded in his quarters, only visiting his father to partake of the evening meal with him. Respectful of his grief, his unit kept themselves busy, carrying out their drills and exercises on their own.

After the mourning period was over Maxim resumed his duties but his heart remained heavy, causing him to wonder if he would ever come to terms with Arun's death or stop railing against himself for being unready at the moment of truth. He, Maxim, had led and Arun followed, because he knew that Maxim would always protect him—except for this one time, when he had failed him utterly. He had stood idly by and allowed Arun's life to be snatched away because he had failed to observe the warning signals that must have been so plainly visible in Khalid's demeanour as he stood in the doorway of the coffee shop. That had been the true test of his soldierhood and he had been cruelly punished for his failure.

Despite Maxim's deep sorrow it was impossible for him to ignore the rumours of an impending French invasion that had circulated in Cairo for months. Lately they had intensified and Maxim was not surprised when Ibrahim Bey summoned all the amirs, the judges and learned men, as well as his military officers to attend a diwan, a council meeting, which would take place at the al-Ayni palace in Cairo three days hence.

On his way to the meeting Maxim sensed an air of subdued excitement hanging over the city as people stood about in knots of three or four, and it seemed to him that while their faces remained carefully devoid of expression, their eyes followed him with a more avid interest than usual. The Cairo rumour mill had obviously operated with its usual efficiency, and Maxim had no doubt at all that these seemingly casual bystanders were already fully informed of the nature of the drama that was about to unfold.

He wondered bitterly whether for him the long-awaited war—for war now seemed inevitable—had not arrived too late. The moment he had waited for, hoped for, dreamed about and for which he had kept himself and his unit in readiness, now seemed almost a mockery of fate. Had fate not already tested his mettle as a soldier and found him wanting?

Inwardly, he knew himself to be changed, because Arun's death had put a human face on killing. He pictured himself now, coming face to face with the enemy on the battlefield. Would he hesitate? Draw his sword too late? Be too distracted by the perception that here, in front of him, stood not an enemy, but a man, somebody's father, son, brother, whose grief would mirror his own, too vivid and too real to ignore? For the first time in his life, he questioned whether he was capable of ending the life of some young soldier, because it meant dehumanizing him enough to treat the taking away of his life as an insignificant isolated incident.

He had believed firmly in the mamluk way of life, which discouraged emotional ties, preferring each soldier to be an island unto himself: to indulge in marriage, children, family life, was to court weakness. The system of recruiting new slaves from outside of Egypt was designed to perpetuate a race of tin soldiers, identical in every respect but unrelated one to the other. They were free to gratify the senses if necessary, but not the emotions, because it would distract them from the purpose at hand, leading to carelessness on the battlefield, and eventually to death.

Foolishly, because he had not taken a wife, he had fancied himself just such an island, immune to emotions such as hurt and pain and love that might distract him from his ambition. Arun's death had stripped away the illusion mercilessly, leaving him painfully aware that his sense of self-sufficiency had been nothing more than an exercise in massive self-delusion.

As he rode up to the palace gates Maxim was gripped by uncertainty, unsure that the road he had travelled for so long was still the one that led to his destiny. Arun's death had forced him to perceive his life from a different perspective, in which all that he had valued so highly now seemed trivial, and the thing that he had lost, irreplaceable.

A hubbub of raised voices greeted him as he approached the council meeting room. He opened the door and paused on the threshold, seized with a sense of alienation. He entered and took a seat near the door and noticed immediately that Murad Bey was present. At the sight of him, any lingering doubt that Maxim still entertained about whether there would actually be a war faded. Only an event of this magnitude would have persuaded Murad to leave his palace. The debate was about to begin and Maxim leaned forward to listen as Murad Bey took the floor.

The announcement that Napoleon Bonaparte had had the temerity to land his troops on Egyptian soil and take Alexandria came as no surprise to anyone. Rumours had been drifting into the capital for weeks now. Murad lost no time confirming what everyone was aware of: that in his opinion the presence of the French army in Egypt was nothing more than a nuisance that must, of necessity, be taken care of, brushed off, perhaps enticed away with gifts, like the proverbial ever-retreating carrot that is dangled just out of the donkey's reach. A small army would be sufficient to accomplish this little task and he himself, Murad declared, would ride at the head of it. As Murad concluded his speech, he looked around the room, sensing agreement, his fiery eyes missing nothing.

When it was Ibrahim's turn to speak a hushed silence fell. It was clear from his expression that he did not share in the unspoken consensus that seemed to have been arrived at so quickly. He was much less certain, he began, that the actions proposed were necessary. If the French were no real threat, why call out the army and march hundreds of miles to confront them. Why not let them come to us? he suggested. They had no understanding of the difficulties of marching through the desert. Very few of them would make it to Cairo and the few who did could then be easily disposed of at little or no cost to the mamluks themselves.

73

The soldiers in the room exchanged uneasy glances, which they let slide as though they were embarrassed to see their thoughts reflected in each other's eyes. It was not the nature of the mamluks to wait patiently like a row of sitting ducks for the enemy to attack, but to rush out enthusiastically to meet all challengers. Ibrahim must know that their style was swifter, more direct. Therefore, the action he was proposing likely had one purpose, and one purpose only: to defeat Murad on ideological grounds, trying to regain control here in the safety of this room, because he must know that he was already too old for the battlefield.

Their unspoken judgement hung in the air and seemed to communicate itself to Ibrahim. His eyes searched the room, seeking support in eyes that would not meet his own, or those that stared stonily ahead, fixed on some point just beyond him. He sat down abruptly, and Maxim knew that a victory for Murad over the French would spell the end of the dual governorship of Egypt.

19

Five days later four thousand mamluks, Maxim among them, with Murad Bey at their head, rode north out of Cairo, departing in forceful waves like a field of flowers being driven forward by a prevailing wind. The long colourful robes which hid their coats of mail, the bright yellow turbans and soft pointed red Turkish slippers lent an air of festivity that was completely at odds with the hostile purpose of their journey. Even their armaments, curved swords, pistols, arrows—inlaid with jewels and intricately worked in gold, silver and copper—seemed more like ornaments than instruments of war. Mounted on their fine Arabian steeds—each of which had cost a small fortune—their saddlebags filled with valuables, the tall, handsome mamluks could easily have been mistaken for a deputation of princely ambassadors, instead of the ferocious killing machines they had been trained to be. Excited and eager, they spurred their horses onward, the drumming of the horses' hooves in the desert sand resounding in their ears like a collective inspirational heartbeat. Following were ten thousand infantry and bringing up the rear were servants to carry the mamluks equipment and to see to their needs.

Behind them the city was in turmoil as the frightened citizens poured out of their homes, loaded with as many of their possessions as they could carry, determined to get out of Cairo while there was still time. Aware of the panic that had overtaken the city Maxim's mood was sombre. Bidding his father farewell had not been easy. Arun's death was a blow from which Qilij had not yet recovered, and Maxim wondered if he ever would. A spare man to begin with, Qilij seemed almost frail now, as though he had suddenly lost a good twenty pounds. And in spite of the fact that he was a soldier, trained to expect the unexpected, he had not succeeded in hiding his apprehension that this might be the last time he would see his second son.

Zainab, who seemed to have taken over the running of the household, reassured Maxim that she would look after his father's welfare. And somehow, that knowledge had set his mind completely at ease. It was odd, he thought. Because of what she had become—which was too westernized for Egyptian taste—her presence in his father's household had brought sorrow. But now, it was precisely because of what she was that he could go off to war confident that under her care, his father's well-being would be assured in her capable hands. And with Khalid dead, no one would be interested in Zainab's whereabouts.

Despite Maxim's sombre mood some of the raw excitement of the occasion began to communicate itself to him. That feeling of pride in being a soldier that he had feared forever lost to him was suddenly reborn. And with that, his military training reasserted itself and his mind emptied itself of all thought that did not concern the job that he had waited years to do. His mind now crystal clear, he mentally reviewed his battle manoeuvres. Finally, it was no longer a drill. It was real.

Couriers had been sent on ahead to spy on the invaders and from the news they brought back, Murad determined that he would meet the French at Shubra Khit, just below the village of al-Rahmaniya on the Nile. Maxim was positioned with his unit on the outside of the left flank. Ibrahim was nowhere to be seen. Baltaa with his forty mamluks spread out behind him was directly on Maxim's right. In war, they shared a sense of common purpose, but Maxim knew that once they rode off the field of battle that solidarity would disintegrate.

His first sighting of the French army was a crushing disappointment. He had anticipated doing battle with equals, not with this disorganized and, to his eyes, shoddily clad bunch of men whose tunics were as unimpressive as those of the best-dressed peasant, and who were disporting themselves like children in the Nile. But then, he argued silently, with their disciplined splendour, the mamluks set a standard impossible for any other army to attain and this knowledge left him feeling more resigned than supercilious. As the call to charge sounded, he experienced a fleeting regret that it would be so easy, and spurred his horse forward.

As the mamluks charged, Maxim realized with some surprise that the enemy soldiers were no longer where he had perceived them only seconds ago. They had fallen into some kind of formation, whereas he had expected them to run around in confusion and panic, and it was he and his comrades whose headlong charge was now in disarray. Horses, some riderless, were wheeling around, turning back into the desert, and his own horse was now rearing, hooves beating the air, instinctively reluctant to continue going forward into the confusion of noisy gunfire and screams of man and beast. Unhorsed riders, weighed down by their heavy armour, stumbled about, only to fall again as the French artillery took unerring aim at these very easy targets.

"Retreat! Retreat!" Men's voices took up the call on all sides and Maxim responded instinctively. He jerked on the reins, turning his mount sharply left in a narrow semicircle and then urging it forward in flying leaps over the obstacles in its way, a melee of prostrate and thrashing bodies of men and horses whose blood was already disappearing into the sand as their erstwhile companions retreated in a headlong flight back into the desert from which they had so proudly emerged such a short while ago.

At the village of Jibbrish a few miles upstream they stopped to take stock of their losses. It was a painful accounting. The advance force had been decimated, reduced to less than half, and out of these, Maxim could only account for four of his unit. Leading his horse by its bridle, he moved closer to where a war council was already assembled around Murad to plan their next move. Baltaa was part of the circle and Maxim noted with grim humour that destiny might be keeping the two of them alive to resolve their unfinished business before they moved on to their next lives.

He realized with some small sense of surprise, not untinged with admiration, that Murad was far from ready to admit defeat, despite the urgings of two of the generals. Undismayed by the turn of events, which he ascribed to bad luck, Murad was proposing a renewed attack on the French who, he felt certain, would assume that by now the mamluks were well on their way back to Cairo.

In his heart, Maxim seriously doubted it. After the initial surprise, it had quickly dawned on him that the French army had executed a brilliant strategy that had rendered them almost invincible. In the midst of the confusion, his mind had registered that their infantry had fallen into square formations to do battle, and he had the impression that the squares had somehow formed an impenetrable wall where, if the rifles of the first square should miss their advancing targets, the raised bayonets of the soldiers grouped inside each square would be waiting to finish the job. Luck, he felt, had nothing to do with it! The mind that had conceived such a brilliant strategy, that seemed perfectly designed to counter the famous mamluk battle charge, had not operated on guesswork. He had no doubt at all that Napoleon Bonaparte, having studied his enemy, would predict their movements with deadly accuracy.

He opened his mouth to speak, his heart beating faster. He was a comparative junior, owning only ten mamluks, and no longer even that, since six had died in the morning's skirmish. Speaking out in opposition to Murad's decision might be foolhardy in the extreme, but their plan of attack had to be changed, or the earth would be soaked once again with the blood of more mamluk soldiers.

"Then let us prepare for the attack at once," he heard Baltaa's voice say. His tone was even, as though nothing more important than the timing of a social call was being decided. Intuitively, Maxim realized that Baltaa had known what he was about to say and had deliberately cut him off. A rumble of assent filled the air and Maxim bowed to the inevitable, realizing that the moment had passed.

20

Maxim listened as the plan of attack was outlined.
Guns would be positioned along the city walls and the Nile
barricaded by a fleet of sunken boats. His misgivings
returned when he heard the second part of the plan. The
army would be split into two forces. Ibrahim, who had
ridden out to join them when the news of their defeat at
Shubra Khit reached him in Cairo, would defend the road
to the city with barricades that would be set up at Bulaq
on the east bank north of Cairo and manned by a reserve
force of mamluks, fellahin and bedouin, while a large force
of mamluk cavalry would deploy near Embabeh on the
west bank under Murad. Camped south of the cavalry
would be fifteen thousand infantry, composed of Albanian
soldiers and a few thousand fellahin.

Maxim foresaw immediately that this strategy could
only end in disaster and was unable to contain himself any
longer. He raised his hand to signal his desire to speak.
Gradually, the assembled soldiers grew quiet as Murad
regarded him with an air of impatience.

"Speak," he said, somewhat irritably. "What is it you
wish to say?"

"I do not think the plan is a good one," Maxim said "Our
spies have reported that the French are assembling on the
west bank of the Nile. If we position ourselves on the west
bank, we are being extraordinarily accommodating to the
French, sparing them the trouble of having to cross the
river to do battle. Our entire army should be positioned on
the east bank so that the French will be forced to cross the
river. We can exterminate them while they are helpless in
the river and the Nile will run red with their blood as she
carries them back downstream to the Mediterranean."

"Pouf! These are the simple plans of one who is
somewhat naive," Baltaa scoffed, "to believe that the
French will oblige us by reacting as we wish them to. What

79

guarantee do we have that they will be foolish enough to even attempt to cross the river? If our entire army remains on the east bank, I wager they will set up camp on the west bank and stay there till winter, for they are a stubborn people. It is we ourselves who may have to cross the river if we wish to do battle with them and drive them out of Egypt once and for all.

"No, my young friend," he continued, "the French will expect us to deploy our army along the east bank since they themselves are approaching on the other side. It would be the predictable thing to do. What we have proposed contains the element of surprise that is needed if one is to be victorious."

"What was the element of surprise you employed at Shubra Khit?" Ibrahim Bey inquired. His tone was one of polite curiosity, but Baltaa flushed.

"None," he said brusquely. "They surprised us. But unlike our young soldier here, I learn from my experiences."

"You have certainly had more time, if nothing else," Murad said, pausing as the older soldiers guffawed. "I am inclined to put it to the vote and let the council decide," he continued.

Silence reigned for several moments as the council members pondered the choices under the watchful gaze of Murad and Ibrahim. Then Murad spoke again:

"What say you?" he demanded, fixing his eyes on the face of the soldier nearest to him.

"I stand with Baltaa," came the reply, to be echoed again and again as Murad's eyes rested on one soldier after another. The result was unequivocal. Apart from Maxim every soldier had declared for Baltaa, except Murad and Ibrahim Bey, who did not need to vote.

"Then we follow the original plan of attack," Murad announced. His glance passed over Maxim and rested on Baltaa's face:

"Our losses so far have been heavy," he said. "If this plan should fail, it will not be long before you acquire a new experience, from which it may prove slightly more difficult to recover." His face was impassive, but the eyes that held Baltaa prisoner in their semi-hypnotic gaze, reminded Maxim of a cobra poised to strike. In spite of his disappointment at the outcome of the vote, he almost pitied Baltaa.

"The council is adjourned," Murad said, as he rose to his feet. "Prepare your soldiers. We leave at once for Embabeh. When the French arrive we will be waiting for them."

21

Spies brought word to the mamluks that Napoleon had begun to march south and that despite the dangers of heat stroke it would undoubtedly pose to his soldiers, instead of following the river he was cutting across the desert to save time. The mamluks hastened to complete their battle plan, putting soldiers to work constructing trenches and barricades to fortify their positions at Embabeh and at Bulaq.

Maxim had made a decision. From what he had already seen, the mamluks' tactical charge would be as little use against the French as it had been at Shubra Khit. The fiercest fighting would be on the west bank which meant that the Mamluks might once again go down to defeat while half their army looked on from the east bank. By rights, that was where Maxim should be: with Ibrahim. But the thought of standing by while his comrades were slaughtered was simply unacceptable. He had to be with them, fight alongside them even though it might mean dying. He would stay and fight on the west bank because that was where he belonged. He was a soldier and he was prepared to die like one: in battle.

By the afternoon of July 21 the French army had broken through the barricades on the west bank and one hour later the battle was enjoined. As Maxim had feared, known, the mamluk soldiers were outmanoeuvred from the outset. By the time the charge was sounded, it was already too late. The French had somehow managed to position themselves between the mamluk cavalry and the fifteen thousand odd infantry positioned behind them to the right. As the cavalry bore down with swords upraised, the French fired upon them at fifty paces with devastating accuracy while Ibrahim and his forces across the river watched impotently.

The slaughter was worse than Maxim had pictured, even though he had foreseen the inevitable outcome. With his four remaining mamluks and a handful of other soldiers, he broke away from the charge, wheeling his horse to the side of the French battalion, hoping to create a distraction from the rear that would disrupt the intense firing that was decimating his comrades. It was a disastrous move. A second square had formed behind the first, and when they opened fire, Maxim and his soldiers narrowly escaped being trapped between the two squares.

The scene became cataclysmic, as though an earthquake had erupted at the peak of some bacchanalian festival, sending the revellers hurtling into the air, only to have gravity bring them crashing back down to earth. Now they lay limply on the ground, looking like broken rag dolls swathed in bright silks and satins. Maxim pulled hard on the reins as his horse reared back and forth, trampling his not-yet-fallen comrades who were on their hands and knees trying to escape. It was a hot windy day, the swirling sand blinding him while the acrid smoke from the French cannons seared his lungs with every indrawn breath.

His gritty eyes streaming involuntary tears, Maxim managed to spy an opening in the melee and guided his horse towards it, barely noticing the sickening impact of the animal's hooves on shattered skulls and broken limbs as it leapt to freedom. A cloud of dust signalled the road to Gizeh as the surviving mamluks streamed onto it and Maxim bent low over his horse's neck, urging it onward to join them. He glanced back only once. Where Embabeh once stood, flames fanned by the wind were now shooting joyously into the air even as the Nile ran red with the blood of those soldiers who had been shot as they tried to escape by swimming across the river.

Arriving at Murad Bey's palace at Gizeh the mamluks stopped briefly, milling around to take stock of their numbers. Murad Bey was among them. His first act was to place Baltaa under arrest.

"Your advice has been akin to treason," he said to him. "It has cost us many lives and almost ensured our defeat. I will not reward you with a quick and painless death out here in the desert. I will keep you alive until we return in triumph to Cairo. You will join us in the parade, not in glory, but nailed to a plank and paraded through the streets on the back of a donkey for all to witness your humiliation. Once you can no longer be revived from your sufferings, your body will be thrown into the desert, to feed the hyenas and the vultures. Bind him!" he ordered, and Baltaa was immediately seized and bound hand and foot. "See to it that he receives food and water, but only enough to keep him alive."

To Maxim's surprise, there was a galleon belonging to Murad on the Nile near Gizeh and it was loaded with his personal possessions as well as cannons and stores of gunpowder. Maxim wondered whether, despite his tenacity, Murad had anticipated the mamluks' defeat and made preparations to flee. Even though he understood the practical thinking that lay behind such a move he felt a twinge of disappointment in Murad.

Murad ordered the soldiers on board the galleon to set sail south, only to watch in frustration as it soon became moored on a sandbar in the middle of the river. Rather than leave it for the French Murad ordered the men to burn it. Deafening explosions rent the air and balls of fire lit up the darkening sky; Murad never looked back. Astride on his horse he led his forces south and Maxim now rode in Baltaa's place.

22

In the months that followed, Murad led the French on an exhausting chase through the desert. Here, with the advantage of being on familiar ground that was completely alien to their pursuers, the mamluks finally adopted what was for them a new strategy. While the main army continued its quick march south, small detachments would be deployed to turn back and detour around the French, coming in behind them like a swarm of scorpions, delivering the sting of death before slipping away to rejoin the main force. But the French kept coming, undeterred by their losses under the mamluks' new technique of guerrilla warfare.

Inexorably, guided by the signposts of the monuments that had remained undisturbed by naught but the wind since pharaonic times, the mamluks arrived at the frontier of Upper Egypt. The French had pursued them doggedly all the way, so that they were continually obliged to break camp and keep moving on. So close was the pursuit that the mamluks' deserted campfires would sometimes still be warm when the French arrived where they had lately been. Neither army had time to reflect on the grandeur of the ancient monuments that marked their passage. For the mamluks, the significance of each rested on its distance from the next, the number of miles, the number of days and hours it would take to cover. At Luxor, they measured the distance to Edfu; once at Edfu, they calculated again how long it would take to arrive at Kom Ombo and to swim across the crocodile-infested waters to reach the town that lay on the eastern bank. Meanwhile, dressed in their heavy hot tunics, which had been designed for war in colder climates, weighed down by their heavy artillery and supplies, the French struggled on determinedly after them, braving the vicious heat of the desert which, even though it was now winter, they found to be unbearable. Like bloodhounds, they sniffed out the clues left behind by the mamluks and kept coming. Still, by the time they arrived at Assouan, the trail was cold. The mamluks had vanished.

In the ten months since they had fled from Cairo, death had accompanied the mamluks every step of the six hundred miles they had so far covered. One after another, injured mamluk soldiers were dropping by the wayside, to be left there by their companions to die, alone and unmourned, stripped naked by nomads for their clothing, their last earthly possession, since their comrades had already relieved them of everything else of value.

Time and familiarity with the spectacle of death had done its work on Maxim. He became immune to death and as it unhorsed rider after rider, his orders that their horses and their valuables be quickly rounded up were immediately carried out. Each night when they camped, the new totals were tallied and brought to him. Under Murad, whose confidence and vision of a triumphant return to Cairo he now shared, he had rediscovered that single-minded obsession with soldiering that had gripped his entire youth and he admired greatly Murad's complete inability to admit defeat.

Soon, he had become Murad's deputy commander and his evolution to power had been so gradual and sustained that acceptance from the other soldiers, even those much older than he, came almost by default. At night, he sat in Murad's tent, planning the next day's march, the next guerrilla attack on one of the command posts the French had now set up along the river.

It was not lost on Maxim that the long march to the frontier was taking an increasingly heavy toll on the morale of the soldiers. As was normal, when they first rode out to war the wealthier among them had arranged for their families to follow them from Cairo to attend to their needs. The families had set up tents near the fifteen-thousand-strong infantry comprised of Albanian soldiers and a few thousand fellahin militia. This was the second line of defence that had camped south of the cavalry at Embabeh and their fighting skills were in no way comparable to that of the mamluks. It was a given that having routed the mamluks, the French would have borne down with a vengeance on the infantry's camp and slaughtered them. It was unlikely that the families camping nearby had been spared and Maxim was well aware that his soldiers were having a hard time grappling with this difficult reality.

The weeks went by and the mood of the soldiers became increasingly unpredictable. Tempers flared suddenly, with altercations occurring over the most trifling of matters and Maxim knew that without an outlet the soldiers would soon rebel openly. If that happened, and the French caught up with them, they would find the mamluk army in disarray and take full advantage of the situation. Maxim pictured vividly the inevitable outcome of such a scenario: simply put, the mamluks would be slaughtered. It would spell the end of his military campaign and probably his career, and was unthinkable. There was only one way out and he took it.

From then on, whenever they made camp and his soldiers departed to scout out the area, he turned a deaf ear to the screams echoing from the nearby villages, as the soldiers sought and found the objects of their search: women, young girls and boys through whom their frustrations could be temporarily eased before they marched on. To himself, Maxim rationalized that the unfortunate villagers and the mamluk families left behind —who had probably been massacred by the French—had shared a similar fate. They had all become casualties of war.

Early one morning, as they were about to break camp, the news was brought to Maxim that Baltaa had disappeared during the night, along with the soldier who had been detailed to guard him. It appeared that they had taken two of the horses. He received the news calmly.

"We have not seen the last of him," was all Maxim said to Murad.

Maxim did not doubt that Baltaa would survive. Date trees were plentiful and the countryside was dotted every three hundred odd yards with saqia, the huge waterwheels the peasants depended on to water their fields in low Niles. Anything else he desired, Baltaa would take by force, even the homemade dhourra cakes and bouza beer which the peasants would have been pleased to offer. But of one thing Maxim was certain: Baltaa would return, if only to conclude the unfinished business between himself and Maxim. Even though Baltaa was out of his sight, Maxim could still feel his burning gaze.

The mamluks had cut back into the interior and were once again headed in the direction of Cairo, but it was becoming increasingly difficult to take the French by surprise. Scouts reported that they had encamped along the river, with command posts about fifty miles apart and that they seemed prepared for a long stay. They also brought news that the Turks had finally responded to the beys' urgent request for help made over six months ago and had sent a huge army to join forces with the British to drive the French fleet out of the Mediterranean. The French army pursuing the mamluks appeared to have received the same information because the scouts brought fresh news: the French soldiers had turned about and were now heading for the coast. Determinedly, Murad set his course for the Mediterranean, believing the French were now safely in front of him.

But the persistent French had not quite given up the chase. They left one detachment behind and in August 1799 they surprised the mamluks but could not take them. For the next three weeks the two sides fought each other viciously along a stretch of the Nile until early one evening, as Maxim sat with Murad in his tent plotting their next day's strategy, the sound of gunfire rang out so loudly he feared that the French had overtaken them at last. Confusion erupted as men came running from everywhere, sabres drawn for battle. As Maxim leapt onto his horse a stinging pain ripped into his shoulder, the force of it almost knocking him out of the saddle, and he cursed himself for having removed his coat of mail. The impact of the bullet caused his legs to twitch involuntarily and spur the horse which sprang forward and galloped away. Instinctively, his hold tightened momentarily on the reins, but in the next instant they had slipped from his fingers as a sickening wave of pain engulfed him, leaving him dizzy. He bent low, almost prostrate over the neck of his mount, realizing that he was on the verge of fainting. With superhuman effort, he grasped the reins again and barely succeeded in

twisting them around his hand before losing
consciousness.

23

When he came to, the horse had stopped and was grazing on a stubble of brush. He was lying crossways across the horse's neck, his head to the side of it, and as he attempted to right himself, nausea overtook him and he vomited into the sand. When the spasm of retching had worn off, he straightened up, grimacing from the pain, wiped his face and forehead on his sleeve and attempted to take stock of his position.

All around him was absolute calm: that stilled hush that marks the transition from dusk to night, as though the world, awed by the very inexorableness of this occurrence, were holding its breath to honour the passage of another day, the setting of yet another sun. Already, the landscape was beginning to blur and would soon be obscured by the curtain of night. The river lay to his left, and on his right, to the west, immense sand dunes loomed deceptively close. The area looked familiar. Twice in the past few months, the French had pursued them to the frontier of Lower Nubia. His horse must have recognized the trail and had kept moving south until sheer exhaustion had likely brought it to a halt.

Somehow, Maxim had managed to remain in the saddle, his feet resting in the stirrups. His injured shoulder felt numb but as he stirred the blood came coursing back into it and a deep, dull ache began to replace the numbness. He had to find a sheltered spot before the landscape was totally obliterated by darkness. Over to his left he spied a dune that promised shelter. He spurred the horse and rode towards it. It was farther away than he had thought and by the time he reached it, night had fallen with dramatic swiftness, embracing him in its inky blackness.

He dismounted, almost falling out of the saddle as pain shot through his shoulder. He pressed his hand over the wound and felt the stickiness of his own blood. He crawled the last few yards towards the dune and as he reached it, he collapsed into the sand. His horse immediately trotted away but Maxim lacked the strength to whistle to it. He thought he heard the sound of running water, but attributed it to hallucination. Huddling in the shelter of the dune he drew his robe tightly around him and surrendered to pain. As he sank into unconsciousness, the thought of scorpions skittered through his mind, but by then he was past caring.

When next he opened his eyes, a small group of men had formed a careful circle around him and were regarding him in silence from a few feet away. The harsh sunlight was intolerable and he shut his eyes again quickly, unsure whether or not he was dreaming. He shook his head in a vain attempt to clear his mind and regretted it instantly. With the vigorous movement his brain seemed to free-float inside his skull, bouncing around sluggishly like a heavy ball of wet string. Dizzy with vertigo he retched, wracked by the painful dryness of it since he had eaten nothing in over twelve hours, and when it was over, his trembling did not pass. He ground his teeth together in an effort to control it and peered up through slitted eyes at the figure that was directly in his line of vision.

They were Nubians. He was sure of it. But in a style of dress unlike any he had ever seen. The Nubians who came to Cairo to work could usually be recognized by their linen cloaks and distinctive turbans cobbled together out of clean white rags. These men however, wore no clothing except for loincloths wrapped around their hips and leather amulets worn on one arm above the elbow. They were leaning on large shields, which they supported by resting the edges on the ground, and each man was carrying a long spear.

His horse, he thought. He had to find his horse. He swivelled his eyes around and spotted it a few feet beyond the circle of Nubians. He attempted to move into a sitting position, to prepare himself to stand up, but the movement was agonizing. He knew he had reopened the wound in his shoulder and could feel fresh blood beginning to trickle out of it. The ache had returned and in spite of the fact that the sun was high in the heavens, he was shivering. As he attempted to stand up, weakness overcame him. He perceived, in a final moment of lucidity, one of the Nubians moving towards him, spear in hand. He held up his hand in a kind of futile warning gesture and pitched forward unconscious into the golden sand.

Maxim's eyes reopened instantly as an incredible lightness of being bore him upwards and he was bathed in a soft bright light. His soul leapt with recognition.

"Arun!" he cried joyously. "How I have missed you." He floated towards his brother, whose embrace reached out towards him, enveloping him in such warmth and love that he was unaware that the expanse of eternity still separated them.

"How can that be?" Arun said with a loving smile. "I have always been close by. Did your heart not sense it?"

"Until now, your absence made my heart so heavy with grief it became an almost insupportable burden," Maxim replied.

"And you sought to escape it by thinking only of war. But look where it has led you." They both looked down to where Maxim's body lay. As they watched, the Nubian moved forward tentatively, seeming to inspect him as he lay there, covered in sand, his fine clothing torn and stained with his dried blood. Becoming suddenly more assertive, the Nubian seized the purse of gold dinars which Maxim had tied around his waist, and jerked it, so that the cord securing it became untied. The Nubian laid down his spear in the sand and poured the dinars into his hand, as his companions crowded around him in obvious excitement.

"May they live long to enjoy it," Maxim said, laughing. "I hope they will be kind to my horse."

"The horse will be fine," Arun said. He sounded regretful and Maxim looked at him questioningly.

"They will be kind to you also," Arun said. His eyes were full of love and peace. "Your time has not yet come," he continued, in response to Maxim's unspoken question. "You sought to leave your heart behind, hardened as it was against your pain, but when you move forward into eternity, you must do so in wholeness with a heart that is healed, not simply forgotten. You must return to find the way."

"Stay with me!" Maxim cried out. He sensed that something had changed. There was no pain, but the beginnings of a heaviness that signalled descent, as though his spirit were being drawn like a magnet towards his own damaged body that lay on the ground below.

"I will never leave you," Arun said, his voice like the rush of the wind in Maxim's ears.

24

Nubia, 1799

Maxim awoke and gazed wonderingly upwards. As his eyes grew accustomed to the semi-darkness, he realized that he was in a small hut, lying on a mat of knitted palm fronds. He stared up at a ceiling of thatched palms, so tightly and intricately woven together that not even a sliver of light showed through. The hut was so tiny that he was able to inspect the rest of it without even turning his head. He could see that in addition to having a thatched roof, it was circular, had mud walls with no windows, but had openings near the ceiling, a mud floor and a doorway, through which daylight emanated. He turned his face towards the light and met the curious gaze of four or five little brown children, who had stuck their heads into the doorway and were regarding him in silence. Realizing he was awake, they broke into fits of giggles and the heads abruptly disappeared.

The doorway was now filled with the figure of a woman who entered carrying a little bowl and immediately crouched down at his side. She was nude to the waist, except for numerous strands of gold necklaces and strings of beads that hung around her neck and partially covered her breasts. Stupefied, he could only stare at her. Some part of his mind registered that she must be Nubian - he had seen them before. Over the last few years the plague and hunger had driven many of the Nubians off the land and some had come as far as Cairo, desperately hoping to find a way to survive. Maxim knew, too, that in some tribes, young girls did not cover their upper bodies until they were married. But in his world they were clothed, and when they became fertile they were veiled to ensure they remained chaste for their future husband. Never before

had Maxim seen a woman—not even a Nubian woman—
expose her body thus, and despite his weakened state he
felt a flicker of sexual desire.

All at once he was conscious of the fact that he was
staring, although only moments had elapsed since she
entered the hut. Embarrassed, he turned his head aside to
avoid meeting her eyes. To his surprise she reached over
and gently but firmly turned his face forward again. Lifting
his head a little with her left hand she picked up the bowl
which she had placed on the floor and brought it to his
lips. He raised his eyes to her face—there was nowhere else
to look—and found that she was watching him steadily.
Her gaze struck him as almost clinical and he realized that
she was totally unselfconscious and seemed unaware of
the effect of her presence upon him.

He took a sip from the bowl. It was some kind of a
soup, but he lacked the energy to even speculate upon its
origins. It was a strange taste, though not unpleasant.
After a few more sips, he turned his head slightly to the
side to indicate that he had had enough, and she
immediately laid his head back down on the mat and left
the hut.

A few minutes later she returned, this time with a
larger bowl which she laid down on the ground beside his
head. He became aware that he was naked to the waist and
that some type of poultice had been placed on his wound.
This she removed and replaced it with a fresh poultice.
After that, she massaged the area surrounding the wound,
along his arm and shoulder, with some kind of liniment
that initially gave off a foul odour, but gradually faded
away as she continued to massage it into his skin.
Comforted by the massage and lulled by the dimness in the
hut, he fell soundly asleep

When his eyes reopened she was gone. Through the
doorway he could see that it was growing dark. It was quiet
outside the hut, save for the sounds of the night creatures.
Still too weak to sit up, he remained where he was, lying
prone on the mat, thoughts beginning to crowd into his
mind. Had they all gone? Packed up everything they
owned, leaving him to his fate, to recover or die, right here
in this hut? But if that had been their intention why would

they have bothered with him in the first place? His thoughts turned then to the woman who had come to him in the hut. Her massaging had soothed him, lulled him to sleep. Had she gone away with them? Did she leave as soon as he had fallen asleep or had she stayed, keeping watch over him at least for a while? The latter idea pleased and comforted him, but the effort of thinking had wearied him and he drifted off to sleep again.

When next he woke daylight was pouring in through the doorway and he realized he must have slept through the night. He could hear people talking and although what he heard was unintelligible to him, the sound of their voices reassured him that they had not left him to fend for himself. He watched the doorway expectantly and was not disappointed. A few minutes later the same woman entered the hut and administered to him just as she had done the previous day.

Her visits to his hut continued for several days, and as he grew stronger, he found himself looking forward with increasing eagerness to them. His eyes had grown used to the dimness of the hut and he had begun to observe her as she massaged his arm and shoulder. What he saw was pleasing. She was not very tall, but her body gave off an impression of strength and good health. Her skin was smooth and soft in appearance, and its colour made him think of cinnamon. Her features were of a pleasing regularity: an oval face, large brown eyes, slightly elongated nose, her lips full but not overly large. Her hair was twisted into ringlets which she had adorned with colourful beads. He could not guess her age, but her body was firm, with small breasts that moved only slightly as she worked. Her expression was habitually grave and since her first visit she had never again allowed her eyes to meet his. When she touched him, her hands felt cool.

He began to wonder what she thought about, or whether she thought about anything at all, and his curiosity grew until gradually he was obsessed by her. He lay awake at night, alone in the darkness, unable to see even his own hand, and thought about her. The stirring in his groin, so new at first, became a sweet and familiar torture that tore at his gut until, forgetting his injured shoulder, he would turn on his side and draw up his knees, using his hand to soothe the hard throbbing ache. Just before dawn, he would fall into an exhausted sleep, from which he would soon awaken and start counting the hours till she appeared in the doorway of his hut.

His obsession hounded him even in sleep. He thought she appeared one night and lay down beside him on the straw mat. He turned towards her eagerly, his hands caressing the coolness of her skin, cupping the roundness of her small firm breasts, passing downwards over the trim waist and rounded hips. He parted her thighs and buried his face in the mat of hair between them, inhaling deeply, drowning in the taste and smell of her. His mind compared her to a forest: a warm, dark and natural place where he wished to lose himself forever; or a lake that cooled his fevered body, but as he looked up into her face to seek her permission, it was the face of Arun who regarded him gravely, and he woke up with a great cry.

That morning when she came into the hut she looked into his eyes and he knew that she was completely aware of his desire. He even wondered if she had perhaps shared his dream. It seemed to him that she took longer than usual to complete her ministrations and by the time the massage was completed, every nerve in his body was electrified. As she moved to leave the hut, he put his hand on her arm to detain her and she froze.

After a few seconds, she made some sounds that, to him, were unintelligible, accompanied by some little coaxing movements with her head and hands. It quickly dawned on him that she wished him to leave the hut with her. He hastened to comply, raising himself up, but the sudden movement made his head swim, and he almost fell back to the mat. She put her arms behind him, supporting him until the dizziness passed. After a while, with her arms around him for support, he got to his knees and half-crawled out the doorway, remaining crouched there for some time, his face upturned to the sun which blazed down on him like a benediction.

After several minutes, he rose up unassisted to his feet and stood there, trembling with weakness, looking around him. He was in some sort of central compound and he saw now that his hut was in fact one of several apartments bordering the compound. There were only a few people around, women and children only, and they were all looking at him curiously. The children, becoming bolder, ran up to him and backed away again, giggling as if at some tremendous joke.

Wryly, he looked down at himself, realizing immediately what the source of their amusement was. Compared to theirs, his skin was as white as the underbelly of a dead fish, and his arms and legs looked like sticks attached to a rib cage. His beard and moustache had grown so long that he could see it just by looking down. He knew the Nubians were repelled by facial hair. Their men wore only small beards, confined to the underside of the chin. He touched his beard, suddenly wishing desperately for a razor of any sort and the next instant he realized that he had another, even more desperate need. He wondered how he had performed his bodily functions whilst he lay ill and, now that he had found the answer, he was filled with such acute embarrassment he hardly knew where to look.

She must have sensed his mortification because she touched his arm and he understood that she wished him to remain where he was. She went quickly into one of the larger huts in the compound, chasing away the still giggling children. Minutes later she came back, bearing a blue linen galabiyah, which she held out to him like a gift, and he saw that on top of it, sat a razor. With some amazement, he took them from her. She turned and started down a small path leading away from the compound down through the fields, towards a bend in the river. He followed her until just before the bend, she stopped and stood aside. He walked past her and saw that here, around the bend, the water had eddied into an invitingly private little pool. He took off his pantaloons and waded in. Embarrassment at his appearance and the odour emanating from his clothing, which he could now detect, had given him new strength.

After he had bathed, he sat in the sun and set to work on his beard. It seemed to take forever but finally he was done. Sun-dried, he put on the galabiyah and walked back around the bend. She was waiting exactly where he had left her, and when she saw him, she immediately began walking back across the field, returning by the path that led to the compound.

The spurt of energy that his embarrassment had fuelled was rapidly diminishing and the walk back to the hut seemed endless and much more exhausting, since the huts were located on higher ground so they would not be swept away with the Nile's inundations. It took a steady climb upward along the path to reach them. At last they were there and he crawled in thankfully and lay down on the straw mat. Now that he was clean, his nose seemed to have developed a new sensitivity and he could tell that the mat he had lain on before had been replaced. She left him, only to return almost at once carrying a bowl of soup. Desperate to lie down he drank it quickly, stretched out full length and was sound asleep within seconds.

25

Some hours later he sensed her presence in the hut and opened his eyes. She beckoned to him from the doorway and he rose up from his bed at once and followed her out into the sunshine. She led him over to a large hut and stood aside for him to enter. As his eyes became used to the dimness, he realized there were six men in the hut, seated around a low bench. One, obviously the chief, was seated at the far end of the bench, while the other five sat around it, on either side. Maxim stood uncertainly in the doorway for a few seconds, then walked in and sat down at the end of the bench nearest to him, directly opposite the chief.

"Allahu Akbar," the chief said to him in Arabic. "Allah is most mighty, for He has restored your health." At this they all picked up the bowls in front of them and drank deeply. Maxim, after a moment's hesitation, picked up the bowl in front of him. He could smell that it contained bouza, a kind of beer made by the Nubians from dhourra. It had sustained him and his soldiers over the months they had ranged up and down the Nile pursuing their game of tag with the French. The mamluks had adopted Islam as their religion and it forbade the consumption of alcohol, but it was a choice between dying of thirst or possibly dying of dysentery since the river water was contaminated from the dead bodies of soldiers floating in it—a sight that had become commonplace. Now he was no longer thirsty but his circumstances gave rise to another consideration: the need to avoid offending his host. Taking a small sip he laid the bowl back down on the table and listened attentively as the chief continued to speak.

They were Dongolawis who had moved several miles downriver to shorten their annual trip to Cairo, he said. His five sons had left their women and children and gone there to look for work. They were returning home to prepare for the sowing season, when they had spotted his horse on the riverbank. When they found him, they believed his spirit had left him, but then he suddenly showed signs of life. They had taken him on board their muggah and brought him here. He had been sick for many, many days and their sister had cared for him.

"I owe you, and her, my life and my debt to you can never be repaid," Maxim said carefully. "What I have is yours," he continued, hastily seeking to reassure them that the purse of gold dinars which he suddenly recalled they had removed from his person as he lay dying in the desert was theirs to keep.

The purse contained two hundred gold dinars, a gift from his father. It was a mamluk tradition to take valuable items with them when they rode off to war. Convinced of their invincibility they considered war the defining moment of their lives from which they fully expected to emerge covered in glory. A display of wealth expressed their power. Maxim suspected—and this suspicion he kept to himself— that a big part of the reason mamluks encumbered themselves with all their valuables was their fear that it would be stolen if they left it behind: a fear that was no doubt justified since they themselves had probably not come by it honestly to begin with.

The dead mamluks whose valuables Maxim had ordered his men to collect had brought many items of great value with them: jewel-encrusted swords, scimitars and daggers which they would use in battle, and gold and silver jewellery and coin secured about their person and concealed in their clothing. By now, all the collected items might well be in French hands, Maxim thought; he had left it all in his tent the night he was wounded in the surprise attack. As far as he was concerned, the Nubians had a greater claim on his purse of dinars. They were the ones who had kept him alive.

"What news is there from Cairo?" he asked. His obvious eagerness for news from home was disarming and seemed to have its intended effect of conveying to them his patent lack of interest in the fate of the dinars. He observed a fleeting expression of relief ripple over all the faces around the table and knew that his responses had met with their approval.

"The French general Bonaparte has taken over the city," the chief replied, as they all watched him closely. "All of your tribe have left the city. Those who were too slow to depart were put to death, as were any caught giving them shelter."

At the news, Maxim's heart twisted agonizingly and he dropped his head to his chest, struggling to master his emotions. His father was dead! Qilij would have been too old and too frail to escape from the city with only Zainab and the two women to help him and presumably his faithful mamluk Qualub had also been killed. Maxim did not doubt they would have tried to conceal his father and may have suffered grievously for their efforts.

"On their way back home my sons passed some tribesmen who were returning to Cairo from Shendi market," the chief said, as Maxim still did not speak. "They said that many from your tribe, who escaped up the river, have taken refuge at Shendi."

Maxim looked up. His eyes betrayed his pain at the thought of the suffering that must have been inflicted on his father's entire household.

"I will see that you are well rewarded if you take me upriver to Shendi," he said at last in a low voice.

The chief frowned. "The inundation has begun," he said. "Travel upriver against such a current is impossible, even with a strong north wind at our backs. We must wait until the flood waters subside. But then, it will be time to sow the seed and it is only after the sowing that there may be time to go upriver. Yet, it is a voyage that takes many days and once the seed has sprouted we cannot leave the fields untended. Although our fields are small they support many people, especially the Kashef, our king, who exacts so much of our crop in tribute."

"Pray forgive me for being so thoughtless," Maxim said. "My grief over the fate of my father in Cairo has robbed me of my senses." At this, all the men nodded their heads understandingly, in obvious agreement with the notion that concern for family constituted reasonable grounds for claims to insanity.

"By the time the flood waters subside, my strength will have returned," Maxim continued. "I will be strong enough to work with your tribe, sowing the seed. Perhaps in this small way, I will be less of a burden to you, although nothing I do can ever repay the tremendous debt I owe to you for saving my life."

"It is my daughter who saved your life," the chief responded, his frown disappearing. "She has been blessed by Allah with the gift of healing the sick by using certain plants as medicine," the chief continued. "While your spirit ranged far from your body, she tended you, applying the poultices that drew the poison out of your wound and feeding you drops of water to sustain you; your body was weak from the loss of blood and from the fever that ravaged you after you were exposed to the chill of the desert night in your weakened state."

"Allah has indeed favoured me," Maxim replied.

There was a brief pause. Then:

"My daughter is in need of a husband," the chief said, and Maxim was immediately aware that the five brothers had intensified their scrutiny of him. "We fear that the next time the Kashef claims his tribute, he will ask for her hand in marriage. If he does, then we are indeed ruined. When the Kashef takes a new wife, he soon begins to demand that her family shower him with gifts and his demands do not cease until the family is totally impoverished."

He paused for a moment, then produced Maxim's purse of dinars and passed it to him across the table. "Your bag of gold has been in my safekeeping while your spirit wandered. Take it." he said, pushing it across the bench towards Maxim. He fell silent and folded his arms across his chest.

At that, the whole purpose of his interview became crystal clear to Maxim. The six pairs of eyes remained fixed on him, and he knew that depending on his response, he would either leave this hut with a wife, or begin a journey alone that, not having fully recovered from his recent illness, he could not possibly survive.

Nubia had been part of the mamluk empire for centuries and Maxim's military education had familiarized him with the geography of Lower Nubia. This knowledge

103

had proved useful during the long months of hide and seek with the French up and down the Nile. The French had pursued the mamluks doggedly, pushing them to the Nubian frontier. Their relentless pursuit forced Maxim to raise with Murad the possibility that the mamluks might have to cross the frontier and penetrate deep into Lower Nubia, where Maxim's knowledge of the terrain would give them a significant advantage over the French. On several evenings Maxim had spent long hours in Murad's tent, working with him on a strategy for eluding the French and mapping the mamluk army's route in the event they were driven into Lower Nubia. He recalled the topography vividly and knew it would be daunting even under perfect conditions. In his weakened state undertaking such a journey alone was unthinkable.

Based on what the chief had indicated, Maxim thought their village was likely situated well north of the third cataract of the Nile. From here he would therefore have two options: he could head north back to Cairo—and in view of why he had left it in the first place returning would be foolish in the extreme—or he could go south in the hope of eventually making his way to Shendi where, according to the chief, others of his kind now lived.

Even as he thought them through, he recognized that neither option was feasible. The location of the village meant that it was in the region of the dreaded Batn el Hajar. The name meant the "belly of rock" and it was apt. Lying between the second and third cataract, Batn el Hajar was where the Nile narrowed, flowing swiftly through gorges whose granite walls rose thousands of metres high on either side, separated here and there by a series of pockets and small plains where tiny villages clung to the riverbank, barely eking out an existence. In some areas it might therefore be possible for him to stay close to the river but when the terrain became impassable, it would mean detouring inland several miles into the desert before returning to the trail along the river again. And even if by some miracle he survived the long trek, he would be seized and put to death by the French as soon as he set foot in Cairo.

The alternative—to go south—seemed equally hazardous. He would be journeying into Upper Nubia. Maxim's knowledge of that territory was limited to awareness that it was a connecting link along the trade route between Egypt and Ethiopia—for textiles, ivory, spices and slaves—thus making it an important contributor to the generation of mamluk revenue. Maxim had never studied its topography in detail because, other than passing through it on plundering expeditions, Upper Nubia had been a part of their empire the mamluks had left largely unexplored. Given the current state of his health, this was not the time to be a pioneer, Maxim thought ruefully.

So, it is settled, he said to himself. There was no question of his undertaking an arduous journey at this time. He would never make it. If he wanted to stay alive— and he did—there was only one alternative left. He had to take the chief's daughter as his wife.

The irony of his situation dawned on him as he recalled his vow of celibacy, proscribing all, whether Circassian, Greek, Turk, Egyptian or mamluk, and he could almost hear the mocking laughter of those who might have thought him too proud, too ambitious. But even as he recoiled from it, a little flame sprang to life deep in his groin, and his blood began to run warm and quick with the knowledge that that very night, the woman with whom he had become obsessed would lie down beside him.

Placing his hand on the purse of dinars he pushed it back across the bench.

26

It was twilight when Maxim emerged from the chief's hut and returned to his own quarters. He sensed that the woman did not immediately follow him. He removed his galabiyah and lay down on the angareeb, his heart pounding with anticipation. About twenty minutes elapsed and it grew dimmer inside the hut. Then a shadow darkened the doorway, blotting out the last lingering traces of dusk as she approached the angareeb and stood over him. Desire made him suddenly impatient and gave him new strength. He reached up and caught her by the waist with both hands, pulling her down to him. As her breast brushed his face, he reached for it instinctively and she reared backwards in sudden panic, pushing his face away in a desperate attempt to break free.

She fought silently, gasping as his mouth closed possessively over her breast. He felt lightheaded with delight at its softness. She stopped struggling for an instant, which he mistook for a sign of willingness and relaxed his hold on her in order to caress her. She immediately seized his hair, pulling savagely as though she would tear it out by the roots and he winced. With one strong movement, he turned over, carrying her with him, and laid her down on the mat, spreading her arms wide and pinning her down. Using his lower body he forced her legs open and both of them cried out as he drove himself deep inside her.

They lay still momentarily, as though equally stunned by the shock of his brutal entry. She recovered first, twisting her body to escape from under him, and with her movements, an amazing warmth began to spread through his loins. Instinctively, he responded, keeping her there, unknowingly massaging her pain. Gradually, her struggles subsided. Slowly, her arms came up around his neck and she pressed her body into his, drawing him deep into her very centre, where her fire raged up to meet him, and he revelled in the newness and wondrousness of it all.

When he awoke in the morning, she was gone. He lay there idly contemplating the intricate pattern of the thatched roof, experiencing a sense of peace and fulfillment of body and mind that was completely new. Three times the previous night he had awakened and reached out to draw her closer, as though he feared she might slip away while he slept. In his mind he marvelled at how quickly knowledge of each other had come, so that the second time their bodies were joined, their mating had been long and intense, filled with moments of shuddering stillness as they fought together to delay the quickening. When it could no longer be held back they raced to release it in explosive consensuality.

Unlike him, she made no sound, but her body quivered powerfully under his and the awareness that he had been the first to penetrate her cool exterior pleased him. The memory of it stirred him now and he moved restlessly on the mat, feeling suddenly impatient. Completely unaware that he was now enslaved he got up, put on his galabiyah and went outside the hut to look for her.

She must have been watching for him, because as soon as he stepped outside, she emerged from one of the larger huts and motioned to him. He crossed the compound and walked into the hut. It was cool and bright, lit by the sunlight that poured in from oblong windows that had been cut out of the mud walls. It was obviously some kind of communal room. It contained several pieces of furniture, chairs and tables, whose seats and tops consisted of split palm branches stretched over a wooden frame supported on four wooden legs, exactly like his bed.

Four or five large earthen jars stood along one wall. From one of these she now took out a woven mat and placed it on one of the tables, then left and went outside. He divined that she was about to serve him breakfast and promptly sat down on a bench in front of the table, realizing that he was extremely hungry. She returned in seconds bearing an earthen bowl from which steam was still emanating, and handed it to him. It was some kind of barley soup and he consumed it ravenously along with the flat round dhourra cakes, still warm, that she had placed before him. She remained standing in the doorway until he was almost finished, then disappeared again, returning this time with a cup of coffee which she set before him and took up her position once more in the doorway. He assumed that they were now considered to be married, attributing the lack of ceremony to the chief's desire to keep his new wealth secret by avoiding attracting even a passing attention from the Kashef for as long as possible.

He watched her reflectively as he sipped his coffee. She was completely enveloped in a long black robe and he imagined that tribal custom required married women to cover their bodies. Her hands and feet were small and delicately formed; deceptively so, he thought ruefully, recalling the painful scratches she had inflicted on him the previous night. He saw now that her features were more aquiline than he had realized and surmised that part of her ancestry was likely Arab. He suddenly became aware that she was watching him watching her and as their eyes met, he thought he detected a glimmer of a challenge buried deep in hers. As he stood up, however, she fled from the doorway unceremoniously and disappeared.

He thought she had gone into one of the other huts and he wandered around, looking into each one. The compound appeared to be totally deserted and he finally made his way down to the water's edge. On his way there, he passed several of the women, the children in tow, obviously returning from doing their washing in the river. Almost all, even the youngest, bore jars of water on their heads. They greeted him with smiles and as soon as they passed by their chattering broke out again. It was a language he did not understand, but they were obviously amused by whatever they were saying. He could hear their laughter, shrill and high, as they made their way up the path.

Arriving at the little pool to which she had brought him the previous day, he performed his ablutions and sat down on the river bank, seeking shelter from the sun in the scanty shade of a fringe of date palms. It was a splendid day, and all the creatures of nature seemed to have emerged to enjoy it. A pair of wild cranes skimmed effortlessly along the water, easily avoiding the snap of an ambitious crocodile. Fish were plentiful, slapping the water as they darted out of reach of the cranes and egrets for whom the gently rippling waters of the little pool provided fertile fishing grounds. Soothed by the sounds of nature and warmed by the sun, Maxim drifted off to sleep.

27

When Maxim awoke, she was leaning against the trunk
of a date palm, watching him. The sun had moved closer to
the west and he realized that he must have slept for over
three hours. He wondered how long she had been there,
standing guard over him. He felt refreshed, though he
realized that his strength had not fully returned. He
beckoned to her and she came over and sat down next to
him on the bank. He took her hand.

"Maxim," he said, pointing to himself. He saw that she
understood immediately. She repeated his name, shyly, a
ghost of a smile on her lips. He nodded yes and pointed to
her, his face questioning.

"Mayya," she said. She gave him a shy smile, showing
small straight white teeth.

"Mayya," he repeated. He played with her fingers,
noticing that her nails were well-kept. On an impulse, he
lifted her hand and kissed her palm, touching his tongue
to it. It was a surprisingly erotic gesture and the strength
of its eroticism must have startled her. She attempted to
withdraw her hand, but he held it tightly, and with his
other hand, caressed her cheek. It seemed to mesmerize
her and her eyes became large and black as she gazed at
him. He leaned forward and kissed her mouth. The breath
from her parted lips felt warm on his own and he drew her
down into the sand, sensing that her eagerness matched
his own. He cradled her head with his left arm and with his
right hand, bunched her robe up between them and
slipped easily inside her. A spasm of desire gripped them
both and the creatures of the riverbank listened in hushed
awe as their rhythmic cries of passion mounted to a
crescendo that shattered the stillness of the late afternoon.

28

By late November, the waters had receded and the planting season got underway. Except for the few women who would remain in the compound to prepare food, every man, woman and child in the village was pressed into service, fanning out into the fields every morning at daybreak. Maxim's strength was returning fast, but he still tired fairly easily and every now and then he would be forced to retreat to the rakuba which had been erected at the edge of the fields. By the middle of the day the food would be brought to them and they would congregate in the shade of the rakuba's thatched roof to eat.

Once the planting was accomplished, everyone took a well-deserved break. Even the tired oxen which had turned the water wheel twenty hours a day seemed to wear permanent expressions of relief as they soaked themselves lazily in the Nile. The hiatus would only last until the tender young shoots began to appear, which would be in about a week. Then, there would be watering and weeding and constant vigilance for the pests that could eliminate the entire crop in a single rapacious night.

During this period of relaxation, Maxim amused himself by teaching the children to count in Turkic and to say everyday words and phrases. More often than not, they would laugh themselves into hysterics at their own and their playmates' efforts. Soon, he became a favourite with them and they besieged him constantly until, sensing when he had had enough, Mayya was obliged to send them away.

He was quietly amazed at his own evolution. His attitude towards the Egyptian peasant had been firmly grounded in mistrust, yet in a few short weeks, he had grown used to the Nubians and moved around the village with an unaccountable feeling of belonging. They were unlike the Egyptians, whose thoughts always seemed to be hidden behind a curtain of deliberate civility that frequently bordered on insolence.

The Egyptian peasants worked the fields reluctantly, unwilling to do more than was absolutely necessary to meet their quotas. The Nubians, on the other hand, tended their small fields assiduously, working from dawn to dusk to wrest a livelihood from the uncompromising land. Yet, they were open and friendly, and although throughout history many of his forbearers had descended upon theirs in a pillaging fury, they had displayed only kindness towards him.

But his people had never stayed long among the Nubians. After plundering and subjugating them, they had returned north where for almost five centuries they had settled on Egypt like a permanent blight. Maxim now realized that in taking control of Egypt, he and his kind had robbed the Egyptians of something precious, the ability to hold up their heads with pride and to look with eyes that spoke their thoughts fearlessly. The coming of the French had precluded the inevitable: the fiery implosion of the love-hate relationship linking mamluks and Egyptians from which, by sheer force of numbers, the new Egyptian might have arisen victorious, like a phoenix from the ashes.

Nature had favoured the Nubians, albeit perversely, endowing them with an environment so hostile that the foreign invaders, including the mamluks, had declined to inhabit it for any extended length of time. Between invasions, the Nubians walked as free men, matter-of-factly pursuing survival, unburdened by the permanent presence of the oppressor that had warped the Egyptian soul.

The need to ensure their survival consumed all their energy, all their days, and was of such overriding importance that for them to have had any other ambition would have been miraculous, unrealistic, even inappropriate. At night, they slept soundly, secure in the knowledge that they shared a common purpose and that there was no enemy within. Astutely, Maxim realized that their serenity hid from view the fact that theirs was the hardest work of all.

There were exceptions, he noted. His wife Mayya, for example, seemed to enjoy some special status, even more than would normally be accorded the daughter of a chief. As he became more familiar with their language, he realized with amusement that the bride price he had paid for her had elevated her almost to the stars, as far as the village was concerned. A Dongolawi bride was normally valued at thirty-six dirhems, a chief's daughter or sister perhaps a little more. He had given a purse of two hundred dinars in exchange for Mayya. Even an Ababda girl, with her Arab beauty, would only fetch six camels, a sum which now seemed paltry compared with Mayya's bride-price that would support the entire village even if the next twenty years were cursed with low Niles. But Maxim wasn't about to complain: he was definitely getting his money's worth.

As his strength increased he spent longer hours helping in the fields and had become wiry and brown, his skin almost as dark as theirs. Mayya seemed to have developed some sixth sense about him and just when he was on the verge of exhaustion she would appear, bearing a drink and nutritious dhourra cakes which he would consume ravenously. At night, her body welcomed him and filled his soul with peace. Gradually, thoughts of Cairo receded from his mind. There was nothing for him to go back to. Nevertheless, he was aware of her watching him sometimes with an unfathomable expression in which there was more than a hint of sadness and he sensed in her an expectation that someday he would leave.

29

Early one morning Maxim was awakened by shrill cries and his first thought was that the village was under attack from a neighbouring tribe. Snatching up his sabre which had lain unused in a corner of the hut for several months he rushed to the door, only to find that the compound was empty. The cries were still rending the air and he ran towards the fields, his heart pounding both from the unaccustomed exertion and from the adrenalin rushing through his body. As he approached the fields, he stopped short, staring in complete amazement at the scene before him. Thousands of sparrows had descended on the fields, perching like some virulent disease on the green stalks which shook visibly under the voracious onslaught.

As the villagers, shouting unintelligibly, beat the fields with blankets and pounded on drums, tins, pots, anything that could serve as a noisemaker, the sparrows rose up like a thick cloud of dust, only to settle again a few yards away and resume their feeding frenzy. Dropping his sabre, Maxim seized a blanket that was lying on the ground and waded into the fray. It took about ten minutes, and then the birds, as though obeying some secret avian signal, rose up as one, winging their way south to the hoarsely triumphant shouts of the villagers.

As the women and children streamed back to the compound, Maxim, the chief and his sons sat down under the rakuba to discuss the next undertaking. The damage to the crop was considerable, they all agreed, but unless the birds returned before the harvest it would still be a successful season, with reason enough to start out on the long trip to Shendi market where the dhourra and barley would be sold and necessities purchased to see them through the next year.

Maxim felt that he had become one of them, sharing in their trials and tribulations, their anxiety over possible crop failure, and their never-ending struggle for survival. He recognized in them a capacity for endurance, a determination to rise again the next day and begin the battle anew that, in its own way, mirrored the mamluk philosophy while enlarging for him the definition of true soldierhood.

The mamluks' engagement had lain with others like themselves; the Nubians, however, faced more overwhelming odds: their battle was enjoined against nature herself. And he was now joined to them. He had eaten, worked, fought and slept with them. One of their women had healed him, body and soul, and she was now as necessary to him as the air he breathed. After seven months, this had become his life and he dreamed of no other. Still, the thought of visiting Shendi, where it was said others of his kind now lived, filled him with unexpected excitement.

30

One month later, the harvest was completed and Maxim and his brothers-in-law prepared to leave for Shendi market. The prospect of his absence for many weeks seemed to add a new, deeper dimension to his lovemaking with Mayya. The last night, after they had made love, she told him that she was now carrying his child. He received the news with mixed emotions. During the months since they had become husband and wife they had talked about many things: the state of his health, this year's crop, water levels, a member of the tribe who had fallen ill and whom she had cured—all the minutiae of daily life. But not once had they talked about having a child.

He realized that on some level they must have both known that it could and probably would happen. He had an idea why he had never broached the topic. It wasn't part of the culture in which he had been brought up. Absent a hereditary tradition, raising families was not a mamluk priority, though there were many who had grown very fond of their women and the children they had fathered. His own father was an example of that. Still, the knowledge that Mayya was expecting a child filled him with an unexpected sense of accomplishment.

All the same, he wondered why she had never expressed any desire to have a child. Did she perhaps feel that for him it would not be so important? From the beginning he had sensed in her a fear that someday he would leave, return to his people. Did she believe he would regard the child as an unwanted flesh and blood link, one that would hold him back once he had decided it was time for him to move on?

Wanting to reassure her he drew her back into his arms. Instead of settling into his embrace she lifted her head to look into his face.

"Does this news please you?" she asked.

"Of course," he replied. "When will the child be born?"

"I think early in the new lunar year. I hope it will be a girl," she added.

"Why not a boy?"

"Because a girl will always have her mother but a boy will need his father."

He studied her face, understanding that her feelings were precisely as he suspected. She had just voiced her fear that one day he would return to Lower Egypt, to his real life.

"Ah!" he said then. "I see. What you really mean is that you think the day will come when I will leave you, never to return."

She made no reply.

"Then in that case I will not go to Shendi," he said decisively, "so there will be no need for you to fear that I will not come back."

Instead of replying she looked deeply into his eyes as though trying to see into his soul.

"You must go," she said at last. "There is always danger of one kind or another along the route. My brothers are counting on you because there is greater safety in numbers. You do not need to be here for the birth; there is nothing you can do. The women will take care of it."

"Are you certain? Because I do not want you to worry."

"I am sure," she said softly.

"Then is there anything I should do for you before we leave?"

"Like what?" she inquired, smiling.

In response he pulled her hard against him, turned them both over so that she was beneath him, and entered her. This time their lovemaking seemed to go on forever, like a slow and intense rediscovery, becoming quick and urgent until her head would lift, neck arched, face buried in his shoulder, locking him deep within her in a kind of rigid spasming passion, until he was completely spent. Then she stroked him, her hands trailing warmly along his body, rekindling his desire time after time until finally, there was nothing left but the need for sleep.

Maxim and his brothers-in-law had departed the following day. They loaded up the four camels owned by the village with sacks of grain and skins of water, and set out in the coolness of early dawn while the mist still clung to the river. The trip would be long and beset with danger from nomads who ranged the desert constantly on the lookout for spoils.

The brothers had decided to take the overland route. As they explained to Maxim experience had taught them that travel by river could be unpredictable, hazardous, and slow. At times the boats were becalmed by the absence of wind to fill the sails; at other times going upstream against a strong current could well-nigh prove impossible. And then there were times when the water levels were so low it was necessary to drag the boats manually over rocks in the cataracts' narrow channels, frequently damaging the boats in the process. Despite the risk of encountering hostile bedouins, the overland route would shorten the journey by three to four days.

They made their way south on horseback for several miles along the east bank of the river and then just north of the third cataract struck out across the Nubian Desert, heading east toward the peninsula formed by the Nile when it reverses its northbound trajectory and begins to flow southwest.

The barren desert landscape, devoid of oases, made the days seem endless. Each day they would rise at dawn and huddle around a little fire, drinking coffee and eating the dhourra cakes the women had packed for them, supplementing their meal with a handful of dates. Then they would set out, travelling until the blistering sun forced them to halt. They would eat their midday meal under a makeshift tent and rest. In the late afternoon they would resume their march, wetting their throats sparingly from their reserves of water, continuing on until utter darkness descended and forced them to stop for the night. Seven days later they arrived at the peninsula.

At the tip of the peninsula the Nile ran wide, deep, and smooth as it turned about. In the far distance Maxim could see the feluccas skimming across its surface like toy boats, their sails swelling in the breeze exactly as they might have

done in pharaonic times. The sight filled him with a
strange yearning, like a remembrance of things past: his
boyhood days when he and Arun had spent hours sailing
on the Nile. Suppressing a momentary urge to weep he
shook his head dismissively and forced himself back to
appreciating the present.

From this point on they would travel south along the
Nile, toward their next stop: Berber. The journey would
take eight more days. The brothers assured Maxim that
this part of the trek would be much more enjoyable. They
were just past the midpoint of a much-used trail that ran
through the desert in a south-easterly direction from Wadi
Haifa near the Egyptian border to Berber. The trail lay
between the desert and the cultivated fields that lined the
river banks. After so many days crossing stony and arid
terrain, the greenery along the route was a relief to
Maxim's eyes and infinitely restful.

As they made their way south toward Berber little
villages and hamlets, hardly more than clusters of mud
huts, came into view occasionally seeming so unchanged
by time that Maxim wondered idly how it was that the
commerce up and down the river had had so little impact
on the bucolic peace and harmony that prevailed in the
upper reaches of the Nile. It was almost as though the
inhabitants, man as well as beast, had long ago silently
agreed to eschew civilization, with some intuitive
awareness that for them, in the final analysis, it would
prove to be irrelevant.

An atmosphere of merriment and depravity greeted
them when several days later they finally arrived at Berber,
a town of mud huts that was, Maxim realized, an
obligatory stop for the caravans wending their way to and
from Shendi. He smiled in amusement at the light-hearted
antics of the Abyssinian slave girls who, making a great
fuss of his blue eyes, rushed to demonstrate their
eagerness and ability to take care of him for the night. He
shook his head with pretended regret, and they moved on,
chattering gaily amongst themselves, ready to display their
charms to the next arrival. Maxim couldn't help noticing
that even Berber women who were clearly neither slaves
nor prostitutes moved about freely in public, chatting with

both men and women alike, their faces unveiled. This surprised him since the Berbers spoke Arabic and he had assumed they were Muslims.

Judging by the cultivated fields of dhourra and barley, of wheat, beans, and tobacco, and the herds of sheep, goats, cattle, and various fowl that Maxim had observed on their way into the town, Berber was very fertile country, well capable of producing more than enough food to support a goodly population and to trade. The town was bustling with commercial activity but Maxim's first impression was that the biggest bargain on offer seemed to be women—principally the slaves, of whom there were many. Cotton, fine horses and camels could also be purchased but to Maxim the price of everything—save for the women—seemed quite high. Apparently the brothers were of a similar opinion, advising Maxim that they would get better value for their grain at Shendi.

Maxim and his brothers purchased some hot food—a welcome change from dhourra cakes and dates—and sat down on crude benches near the vendor's shack to eat. They ate quickly as the sun began to cast long shadows. Twilight was approaching and they needed to find somewhere safe to spend the night. They found a sheltered spot next to a lean-to on the edge of a field. After tending the animals they bedded down for the night. As a precaution, they slept sitting up, in a circle, leaning against their sacks of grain. At Berber, as it would be at Shendi, there was no such thing as honesty among strangers.

31

Even compared to cosmopolitan Cairo, Shendi market appeared like a microcosm of the world, offering every product from gold to salt, and a promise to grant even the most secret desire. After they had found some space to display their goods in one of the stalls, Maxim left his brothers-in-law and strolled around the market place. It seemed that every race on the face of the earth had sent its representative to Shendi and they had brought with them goods to please every taste: silk, cotton, spices and gold, perfume and kohl from the Far East, and perhaps the most precious commodity of all—slaves from Ethiopia.

The peaceful interlude of the last several months faded like a dream as the well-remembered sounds of noisy, aggressive haggling crashed around Maxim's ears, and the market place was transformed into the Cairo souk, a great melting-pot where race counted for naught and superiority was defined by the astuteness of one's bargaining skills.

As Maxim walked by the monkey-seller one of the trained monkeys jumped into his arms and pretended to remove a coin from his ear and he laughed aloud from sheer exhilaration. He scanned the faces of those who were fair-complexioned and bearded, eagerly looking for some sign. Now and again, some bright colourful costume in the distance would catch his eye, and he would stare intently. He had heard that there were some mamluks who had managed to maintain their lifestyles upriver, living luxuriously aboard their boats, attended by slaves. But if there were any in Shendi they must have thought it prudent not to advertise their presence by their dress, because he spied not a single mamluk costume. Disappointed, he headed back to the stall, since night was falling.

The following day, after an uncomfortable night huddling in front of the stall with his brothers-in-law, Maxim set out around noon for another tour of the market.

"I will save you some money by not tending the stall with you," he said to the brothers with wry amusement. "I fear my inexperience at bargaining is written all over my face, and it seems to attract men of extraordinary talent in this field like flies to a honey-pot."

This time he spotted them immediately, in the first bouza shack he entered. Four bearded men, whom he knew instinctively to be mamluks, were seated around a small table in one corner of the shack. Recognition was mutual in spite of the fact that Maxim had long ago shaved off his beard. As he approached the table where they were seated, one of them stood up, his hand outstretched in greeting.

"Welcome, brother," he said, as Maxim grasped his hand. "We know you are one of us. You are safe here, but we use no names in public. Tell us, what news do you bring from Cairo?"

"It has been many moons since I left the city," Maxim replied, sitting down. "These past months I have been sheltered by a tribe of Nubians who came upon me in the desert as I lay dying from the wounds I received in battle, and nursed me back to health. They have told me that Napoleon Bonaparte is in complete control of Cairo."

"So he is. But a caravan that passed through as of late brought news that the Cairenes have grown bitterly resentful of the French soldiers and in retaliation, Bonaparte has passed laws that restrict their freedom in great measure. They dare not disobey or try to cheat him in any way."

"What new laws has he passed?" Maxim inquired.

"His government has intruded into the daily lives of the citizens and regulated them beyond all reason. He has increased taxes and imposed new charges on just about everything. For instance, the people now need the state's permission even to bury their dead and must first purchase a license to do so."

"Perhaps this is why plague has broken out in the city," a second mamluk suggested. "The dead may have been left too long unburied while the Egyptians contemplate how to avoid paying for the licence. As you know, they do not part easily with money."

"It is said that Bonaparte wishes to turn Cairo into Paris-on-the-Nile and all these new regulations and licences are how he will raise the money to do it," said a third. "Some areas of the city are being torn down to make way for new avenues and boulevards where only the French and rich Egyptians will be able to afford to live. The people are forced to keep the lanterns burning outside their houses all night long to beautify the streets even though no one is about, or else they are fined. He even attempted to remove the graves in Esbekiya Square and relocate them to the tombs of our forbearers outside the city, but there was such a hue and cry from the people that he was forced to desist."

"But what truly angers the masses is that each morning, instead of the call to prayer, they are awakened by the sound of a cannon being fired over the city, which they find wretchedly nerve-wracking," the first mamluk said. "There was talk of a jihad if this state of affairs continued. If there is one and the French are driven out of Lower Egypt, who knows, the time may soon be at hand for us to return."

"Should that day ever arrive it is possible that our situation in Cairo will be very different since it appears that our numbers are now greatly diminished," Maxim remarked. "I understood that when Bonaparte took control of Cairo any mamluks who had not fled the city were put to death."

He paused. He had been on the verge of inquiring of these men whether any of them had news of his father but it would mean identifying himself by name, which he did not want to do. Also, his father may have been lucky enough to escape and could be in hiding somewhere in the city. Should he learn that Maxim was alive, he might attempt to send his son a message and in the process inadvertently reveal his own whereabouts. News travelled up and down the river and it was notoriously difficult to keep a secret in Cairo. Maxim decided to hold his tongue.

"If any remained they are in hiding for fear of being denounced by the Egyptians. Few of us have any real friends among them, as you know," the man replied in answer to his observation.

"And yet, you talk of returning," Maxim observed. "I am not so sure that if the Egyptians succeed in driving out the French, they would welcome our return with open arms."

"The French are novices when it comes to dealing with Egyptians, while we have been doing it for hundreds of years," scoffed the fourth mamluk, who up till then had remained silent. "In any event, where else should we go? Cairo is where we belong. We know no other home." His tone was arrogant and sure, containing no trace of self-pity or insecurity. The months spent in exile had left him unscathed, had forced no examination of conscience, and it occurred to Maxim that the sentiments voiced by this soldier were likely shared by mamluks everywhere, as they hid themselves all over Egypt, biding their time until they could return to Cairo, like lions returning to the kill.

It was mid-afternoon before Maxim recollected guiltily that he had completely deserted his brothers-in-law, but five hours had never passed so swiftly. He shared an identity with these men and at first had been fascinated by their accounts of battles that had taken place along the river bank as he lay ill. But then, unaccountably, he grew weary listening to them and suddenly they appeared to him to be pathetic. Maxim stood up abruptly to take his leave. The mamluk who had first greeted him accompanied him as he left the shack.

"I recognized you," the mamluk said to him when they were out of earshot of the others. "You are Maxim Bey. I am Ismael. We had assumed that you suffered the fate of most of the other beys at the hands of the French. You were fortunate. Not many of them escaped."

"How many of our people live here in Shendi?" Maxim asked.

"That I do not know for certain. I would say about forty, but it is only a guess. Some live on river rafts and only come to the market after nightfall, in search of prostitutes or slaves who they rent from the owners for one night. Some brought their women and children with them when they fled from Cairo. Still others have found companions here and are settled with them for the time being." He glanced at Maxim speculatively. "The Ethiopian female slaves are said to be the most pleasing companions. If you are in need of constancy, it would be simplest to purchase one outright. She can be resold for a profit when you no longer wish to keep her."

"Regrettably, my stay in Shendi is of short duration," Maxim replied. "We depart day after tomorrow." In spite of himself, a tinge of coldness had crept into his voice. The callousness of the offer had been unintentional, he well knew. To some mamluks, sexual satisfaction was, after all, only a commodity: to be paid for like any other if it could not be obtained by force or benign persuasion.

Uncomfortable with the notion, he struggled to suppress a sudden feeling of irritation that was accompanied by an overwhelming desire to rid himself of his new companion, who seemed intent on accompanying him all the way back to his stall. He stopped and turned to him:

"Pray do not deprive your friends of the pleasure of your company any longer," he said. "I will say farewell now, since tomorrow I will be occupied with purchases that must be made and the preparations for the return journey." His voice was calm and pleasant, but the natural authority behind it was unmistakable.

The man's eyes narrowed with patent awareness that he was being dismissed, but despite his obvious displeasure he held out his hand:

"Farewell, then, Maxim Bey," he said. Maxim grasped his hand and shook it firmly. Then he turned around and was immediately swallowed up in the crowd.

The following day, he and his brothers-in-law busied themselves making the necessary purchases and preparing the animals for the long trip back: feeding, watering, and checking the condition of the camels and horses. Maxim stayed close to the stall, fully conscious that he wished to avoid the mamluks he had met the day before and having no desire whatsoever to seek out others. Besides, knowing at least one of them had recognized left him feeling uneasy. They had said they used no names. But as Murad's deputy commander, he had played a prominent role in the war against the French until he had been wounded, and had most likely been presumed dead. No doubt the news that he was alive and well was already circulating among the mamluks hiding in Shendi; eventually the rumour would find its way back to Cairo so probably the damage had already been done. To protect his father the best thing he could do now was to keep a low profile and hope that if indeed his father was alive, the news that his son had survived would not reach him.

The following morning they loaded up the camels and set out overland on the return journey. Maxim felt only relief at leaving Shendi market behind. The thought that he had once secretly harboured—of remaining in Shendi with his own kind—had vanished completely. What he had found there had been nothing short of disappointing. He was certain that the mamluks whom he had met were typical of those who had taken refuge at Shendi. With nothing to occupy their minds, no real talents except in the art of war, they had become a dissolute bunch of dreamers, no doubt sitting around the bouza shacks every night until the early hours of the morning, reliving past glories and dreaming of a future when the departure of Bonaparte would leave the way open for their return to Egypt.

There were other reasons why he was now eagerly looking forward to his return to the village. The coarseness of the prostitutes as they openly displayed their wares, slipping their arms invitingly through his, had repelled him, but even as he charmingly disengaged his person from their clinging hands he knew himself to be stimulated with desire, the object of which lay at the other end of his journey.

32

They set out at a good pace, determined to cover as many miles as possible until forced to seek shelter from the sun. As mid-morning approached, Maxim noticed that every now and again one of the brothers would swing around in the saddle to look behind him, his hand shading his eyes from the glare of the sun.

"Why do you keep looking behind us?" Maxim asked him finally.

"We have been followed ever since we left the market," the brother replied.

Immediately on the alert, Maxim turned his horse around and brought it to a standstill. In the far distance, he perceived a rider sitting motionless on his horse and something about his sudden apparition made the hair on the back of Maxim's neck prickle. As he watched, he realized that the rider was not standing still at all but was moving forward rapidly and, although he must have known he had been spotted, making no effort to stay out of sight.

As he approached within thirty yards, he stopped moving and remained seated on his horse, so that he and Maxim now stood still, facing each other.

"Baltaa," Maxim said softly. He felt no surprise, no sense of shock. Just a feeling of inevitability, of being faced with a defining moment that he had known all along would arrive.

"A long spear, quickly," he said to the brothers and the tone of his voice was all the explanation they needed.

For one long moment, he and Baltaa stood still, each silently acknowledging the other as the instrument of his death. Then the pounding of hooves broke the stillness as Maxim and Baltaa urged their horses forward as if in intuitive response to some unearthly signal. Like jousters in King Arthur's court they thundered down upon each other, nerves straining, muscles taut as they took aim, thrusting their lances forward and sideways viciously as they bypassed each other, momentum carrying them on for several yards before they reined in and turned the horses about to prepare for the next charge.

With blurring speed, they raced forward for the second time and Maxim barely managed to whip his head aside as Baltaa's lance whizzed by his face, grazing his cheek. They reined in their horses once more. This time the pause was an infinite second longer and Maxim sensed that death loomed, impatient. One second later, they bore down on each other for the last time and as he approached Baltaa, Maxim leaned forward and thrust mightily. The force of the impact of his lance as it pierced Baltaa's breastbone almost threw Maxim from his horse and the lance was wrenched out of his hand as momentum propelled him forward.

Turning his horse around Maxim saw that Baltaa had dropped his lance and was tugging with both hands at the spear buried in his chest, attempting to pull it out. As Maxim watched, Baltaa seemed to crumple suddenly and fell off his horse, landing with a muffled thud as the blood from his wound gushed into the sand and disappeared.

Blood streaming from his cheek, Maxim remained seated on his horse. He recalled Arun's prophesy that his destiny had been intertwined with Baltaa's. He felt curiously empty, devoid of all passion, experiencing neither hate nor regret nor feelings of victory; as if in killing Baltaa, he himself had also died. After a while, he became aware of the brothers, waiting and watching silently. He rode his horse up to Baltaa's and taking it by the bridle led it away with them. They had not gone many yards when with a flutter of wings a flock of crows appeared and began to circle over Baltaa's body.

33

Their return to the village was greeted with shouts and laughter by the women and children, who ran out to meet them and lost no time in unpacking and exclaiming over the goods they had brought with them.

Maxim observed that Mayya was not among them, but as they sat down in the communal room to eat she appeared. Without meeting his eyes she began to serve him his meal. As the men ate, the women and children continued with their unpacking, filling the room with their noisy excitement as they spread out the lengths of cloth and beads that would beautify their bodies for the next year. Mayya, he noticed, barely glanced at the merchandise, her demeanour remaining aloof.

As soon as the meal was over, each man disappeared into his hut accompanied by his woman. Maxim strode into his hut without a backward glance, lay down on the angareeb and closed his eyes, waiting. For several weeks now, he had fantasized about being with Mayya and now that he had finally arrived, her coolness towards him was like a dash of cold water on his ardour.

The women in his life seemed extraordinarily capricious, he thought, although so far there had only been two, if one could actually count Zainab. Perhaps he should have remained celibate! The signs of Mayya's pregnancy were more obvious, although from what he could see, her body had not changed much in the weeks he had been away. He had heard that when they were in that condition, women were sometimes difficult to manage, especially in the early stages. He opened his eyes and noted without too much surprise that he was still alone in the hut. He forced himself to lie there for several more minutes until, feeling somewhat exasperated, he got up and went outside.

He headed straight down to the river. As he expected, she was there, leaning against a palm tree. He walked up to her and stood in front of her, looking into her face. Her eyes, looking back at him, were black and dewy. Still without speaking, he touched her shoulder, gently at first, and as desire whipped at him, his hand slid down caressingly over her breast. She came alive suddenly, slapping his face with such wild fury that he was momentarily taken aback. He caught hold of her hands and pinned them to her sides, pressing his body against hers to prevent her from moving. She struggled for some seconds, but then stopped, and her body sagged against his, heaving with emotion.

"What is the matter with you," he said to her gently in the Kenuzi dialect used by the village. He had acquired some fluency in the months he had lived in the village because, although the men spoke Arabic which they had had to learn in order to work in Cairo, the villagers communicated with each other in their dialect.

She shook her head without answering, and all at once, he understood. The night before his departure for Shendi he believed he had reassured her that he would return. He saw now that despite that, she still had not expected him to come back and had spent the past several weeks in apprehension that he would decide to remain with his own kind, dreading the moment when her brothers would return without him, making her an object of pity in the village.

She had not come out with the others to greet them because he might not have been with them and there would have been no way of hiding her grief and humiliation from the tribe. Her fury was the expression of her relief. He marvelled silently at her proud spirit, finding it touching. From the pocket of his tunic he drew out the bracelet of Ethiopian gold that he had bought for her out of his share of the harvest and slipped it over her hand. She raised her arm to admire it, smiling tremulously, and he folded his arms around her possessively.

They walked back to the hut together and lay down on the angareeb, conscious that their relationship had moved onto a different plane. For the first time, he removed all her clothing himself, examining her body attentively. He could see now that it had changed subtly, become more defined, her belly not so flat, more round and firm to his touch, her breasts slightly heavier and hot under his palm. He kissed them, touching his tongue to the hard round nipples. He caressed and kissed her body, his hands and lips revelling in the silky smoothness of her skin, the firmness of her flesh. As he kissed her thighs the well-remembered fragrance of her body suffused his nostrils and the scent of it made him want more. He felt her shiver as his tongue explored her and then she was crying out, cries that seemed wrung from the depths of her. His spine tingled at the sound and he experienced a ripple of manly pride that he had pleased her so greatly. When she quieted he knelt over her and looked questioningly into her eyes, so hard with his own wanting that he feared that in her condition he might hurt her. In answer, she lifted her arms and he lowered his body onto hers.

Mayya's pregnancy was uneventful and their lovemaking had proceeded almost into the eighth month. The delivery, as far as he knew, was without complications. That morning, he and the other men had been sent away by the women and had spent most of the day seated in the shade of the rakuba at the edge of the fields, chewing tobacco and playing a game of chess which Maxim had taught them, using crude pieces he had fashioned out of wood.

When they were finally allowed to return to the village, Maxim had a daughter. Mayya had named her Noura. It meant "light", she told him. He gazed curiously at the infant suckling at Mayya's breast. The child was light-complexioned, with brownish hair that curled slightly at the edges, and brown eyes. He thought that she would likely grow up to be a beauty. After a few days, he resumed his lovemaking with Mayya, while Noura slept in a rush basket at the side of the bed.

As was normal for mamluk men, Maxim played no part in caring for the infant. That was Mayya's responsibility entirely and any help she needed was forthcoming instantly from the other women in the village. As a result, Maxim initially experienced no strong paternal impulses towards the child and Mayya did not seek his involvement in what she likely regarded as a woman's job.

34

From early on Noura clung only to her mother. From the safety of Mayya's arms she would watch Maxim as he went in and out of the hut.

"Her eyes follow you around," Mayya remarked to him one morning as she sat on the bed breastfeeding Noura. Maxim looked at her, surprised. Noura was just four months old but to Maxim she was still a tiny baby, a creature who Mayya carried around with her in a sort of sling contraption during the day when she did her chores and who mostly slept and cried when she was hungry, usually—it seemed to him—in the middle of the night: hardly a real person and certainly not one capable of an intent to observe. He glanced down at Noura to find her eyes trained unblinkingly on him. It struck him that there was something perceptive in her gaze and he found it intriguing.

"She looks as though she's thinking," he said, staring back at Noura.

"She is," Mayya replied. "She's thinking about you. She's wondering who you are."

"How do you know that?" he asked, puzzled, gazing at Noura as though really seeing her for the first time.

"She told me," Mayya said, looking amused.

"Then tell her my name is Maxim and that I'm her father," he tossed back, smiling at Mayya as he turned towards the door.

As he made to walk outside Mayya called out to him.

"She wants to know where her father is going," she said.

He stuck his head back in the door for an instant. "Just tell her that by the time I return I will be very hungry," he said wickedly, not answering Mayya's question. He took one last quick look at Noura. Sure enough, her brown eyes were fixed on him.

The following day after lunch Maxim returned to his hut to rest. Shortly after, Mayya followed him in carrying Noura and laid the sleeping child down next to him. Mayya changed her clothes, took down a few of her herbs and medicines from a shelf and placed them together with one or two articles of Noura's clothing in a cloth bag which she tied around her waist and swung it around to her back. Maxim knew she was on her way to tend a woman in the village who was ill. As she bent to pick up Noura Maxim looked up at her questioningly.

"Are you taking her to the sick house with you?" Something in his voice suggested the only acceptable answer and she gave it.

"No. Our sister-in-law will take care of her until I return," she replied.

"She is asleep. There is no need to wake her. Leave her with me," he said, his tone authoritative.

Mayya hesitated, then slowly swung the backpack to her front, removed Noura's things from it and placed them on a low table.

"I will only be gone for about an hour," she told him. "She will probably not awaken, but her teeth are coming in early so she might. Before I leave I will bring you a rag bag for her to suck on in case she wakes and cries. Are you sure you will be able to manage?" she ended, looking worried and slightly perplexed.

"There is a first time for everything," Maxim said confidently.

Mayya readjusted her backpack and stood looking down at him for a few seconds. The glint in her eyes said plainly that he had no idea what he was talking about but she managed not to voice it.

"Fine then," she said cryptically. "I will get the rag bag."

Mayya returned in a few minutes carrying a covered bowl which she handed to Maxim. He opened it and lifted out a long strip of muslin knotted into a little ball at the end.

"How will this stop her from crying?" he asked, puzzled.

"There is dhourra cake soaked with honey wrapped inside the ball," Mayya explained. "Put it in her mouth. The sweet taste will make her suck on it and it will soothe her gums. Hold on to the ends so that the ball does not become stuck in her throat," she warned.

"This is a good idea," Maxim said. He sounded magnanimous.

"It has been around since long before you were born, and your father, too," Mayya responded drily. She shifted her feet indecisively, a fine worry line marking her brow.

"Go!" Maxim ordered. "We will be fine. I have commanded armies. I think I can manage a small child."

"We will see," Mayya said equivocally. "Make sure the bowl stays covered so that the flies and the ants do not get on it," she advised.

Maxim shot her a look.

"Very well," she said hastily. "I am going."

Maxim breathed a sigh of relief as his wife finally left the hut.

He lay next to Noura for a long time on his side, watching her sleep. Every once in a while her eyelids would tremble as though they wanted to open but lacked the strength to lift the heavy dark lashes fanning her cheeks. Or suddenly her leg would kick out reflexively, or she would turn her head away from him and he would stare at the downy hair at the back of her head, willing her to turn around again and face him. Now and again she made little sucking noises and he thought it meant she was hungry. He debated whether to wake her up and give her the rag bag. But then she would grow very still; he could detect no movement at all, not even her breathing. He watched her closely but saw no sign of her chest rising and falling. Nothing. Gripped by a sudden fear that she might have died right there in front of him, he brought his head close to her face and put his ear next to her mouth and nose to reassure himself that she was alive. He noticed she was sweating; her face was pink and he wondered anxiously if she had suddenly developed a fever or was just feeling the effects of the heat. Forty minutes or so later, when Noura's eyes opened, Maxim felt as though he had been holding his breath the entire time.

Noura studied him briefly then turned her head away, looking around, obviously searching for Mayya. Then her eyes returned to Maxim, her face began to pucker, and she let out a wail of distress. Before Maxim could even react Noura's wails were bouncing off the walls of the hut and growing louder by the second. Stunned that something so small could produce such ear-splitting sounds Maxim began to panic. He sat up, reaching for the rag bag in the bowl. In his haste he clumsily knocked the cover off. It fell to the floor and shattered. He snatched up the rag bag and tried to stuff it into Noura's mouth in a frantic attempt to stop her screaming.

Noura made a gurgling sound and horrified that she was choking, Maxim pulled the rag bag out of her mouth whereupon Noura drew a breath and resumed screaming. Her face was growing redder by the second. She appeared to be on the verge of having a seizure and Maxim's panic turned into terror. He had to get help.

Snatching Noura off the bed he rushed to the door, his two hands holding the screaming baby out in front of him and almost collided with Mayya. Calmly, she took Noura out of his hands and walked into the hut cuddling her, and just like that, Noura stopped wailing. To Maxim the sudden silence felt like a blessing. Sheepishly, he followed Mayya in and sat on a bench watching as she fed Noura.

Mayya did not utter a single word until Noura had finished feeding. Then she put Noura over her shoulder and patted her back to force out the air bubbles Noura had ingested while sucking.

"I am sorry, Maxim" Mayya said, cradling Noura, who had resumed her study of Maxim. "I knew it was wrong to leave you alone with Noura and that is why I hurried back. Taking care of babies is women's work. The men of our tribe do not concern themselves much with infants. They have other responsibilities. Their job is to provide their families with the necessities of life by labouring in the fields and marketing what they produce in exchange for the things that we need. They must also ensure there is more than enough to pay the taxes to the Kashef and the poor villages like ours suffer the most because we cannot fight back against his soldiers. It is the men who uphold

135

the honour of their families and who defend the village from other villages who seek to follow the Kashef's example of taking from others by force.

"Women are expected to care for babies and small children and to look after all things that concern the home. At the planting and at harvest time they and the older children help the men because there is much work to do.

"When the time is right, the men begin teaching young boys all that they need to know and it begins very early, sometimes they are but five years old. And women do the same with young girls. The tribe will find you peculiar if you seek to involve yourself in women's work. Do you understand what I am saying?"

"Yes," Maxim replied. "It was the same where I came from." He sounded glum.

"There is nothing to stop you from spending time with Noura in the privacy of our hut if that is what you really wish to do after a tiring day in the fields," Mayya said. Her tone was sympathetic but her expression conveyed that she seriously doubted this would be the case.

"Come and sit next to me. Soon, Noura will become used to being as close to you as she is to me and she will come to you on her own. She will not always be a baby," she added. "In a short time she will sit up, then she will learn to crawl, and I promise you she will not leave you in peace."

Maxim brightened and did as Mayya suggested. She put her hand on his:

"Things will happen as they are supposed to, Maxim. It is best to let nature take its course."

The months went by and Noura proceeded to develop precisely as Mayya had predicted. Many mornings Maxim would open his eyes groggily, awakened by a blow to his head from one of Noura's toys. There she would be, standing at the side of the bed, ready to smack him again to ensure he was fully awake. He would lift her onto the bed and for the next few minutes she would carry on a monologue in baby talk as she crawled from one end of the bed to another, happily trampling all over him in the process.

Soon, whenever Maxim left the hut, Noura would hurry after him as quickly as her little legs would allow, only to shriek with rage when Mayya caught up with her and brought her back. To distract Noura when Maxim was leaving Mayya would give her a toy but as soon as Maxim started for the door Noura would drop the toy and hasten after him. Finally, it was Maxim who put a stop to this. One morning before leaving he sat Noura down on a bench and kindly but firmly told her she was not to cry or run after him.

"If you are good, I will bring you something," he promised. "Will you be good?"

She nodded. Her eyes held tears but they did not fall and he was proud of her. That evening he brought her a wooden bird that he had carved during his lunch break and Mayya promised Noura she would help her to paint it with dye the next day.

As Noura passed the toddler stage she was allowed to play outdoors in the central courtyard with other children of the village. When she showed them her beautiful bird that Maxim had carved, they besieged him to make some for them as well. In his spare time he would sit outside the hut surrounded by them as he carved the little toys that made them so happy to own. He was entertained by how possessive of him Noura became. She would assert her right to be the one closest to him by simply pushing away any child who encroached on what she clearly regarded as her territory.

He realized Noura was very intelligent. He had taught her Arabic and Turkic words and she used them proudly, looking at him for approval as she played. At bedtime, she would climb up on the bed to lie between him and Mayya and would usually fall asleep with her head on his chest.

When Noura was almost five Mayya entrusted her with a little task to do for her father. While Maxim worked the field in the blazing sun, it would be Noura's job to bring him water from time to time. This was a task commonly given to the children of the village. With an air of responsibility about her, Noura would sit in the shade of a rakuba, watching him. When he appeared at the edge of the field she would go to meet him, carefully holding a dipper full of water to avoid spilling it. When he was through for the day she would take his hand on the walk back to the village.

Then one day, his work completed, he approached the rakuba to find her curled up on the bench fast asleep. She did not waken when he picked her up and began the walk home carrying her. Her little body was cradled against his, soft and warm and damp. Her head lolled on his shoulder and impulsively he buried his nose in her hair. It was like breathing in the scent of a rain-washed leaf. Without waking she turned her head around so that her forehead now pressed into his cheek and at the same time, one little arm came up and slid around his neck.

In that moment Maxim experienced an epiphany. His heart seemed to turn inside out and his hold on her tightened reflexively. From one second to the next, he had gone from simply loving his child to knowing that he would give his life for her. He strode into his hut and laid her down carefully on the bed so as not to awaken her. For a few seconds he remained bent over, studying his sleeping daughter through new eyes. He straightened up to find Mayya watching him from the doorway. She must have seen them returning and followed them to the hut. They exchanged a long look and he saw that she knew what had happened to him: infinite paternal love had pierced his heart.

He stood there—sweating from his long uphill trek carrying Noura—and watched his wife. She knew he was tired and hungry but his eyes spoke of a different and more pressing need. She entered the hut; her hands already busy undoing the fastenings of her clothing. Three steps and he was with her, drawing her down urgently onto the marital bed.

Inexorably, Maxim's destiny was being irreversibly altered. He had established a new life among the Nubians. He spoke their language, ate what they ate, worked alongside them in the fields. With his marriage to Mayya and the birth of Noura, he had put down roots, started his own dynasty. His assimilation was almost complete and he was content that it was so.

35

With the windfall of dinars that Maxim's arrival had brought, the brothers no longer made the long trip to Cairo to look for work that would have kept them away from the village for many months. They preferred making the shorter trip to Shendi market each year to trade.

Although haggling over dirhems wasn't his style, Maxim had become adept at driving a hard bargain, earning the grudging admiration of the traders who now knew better than to entice him to their stalls as he walked through the marketplace. He never again saw the mamluks he had come across on his first trip to Shendi and assumed that for whatever reason, they had moved on.

Each trip to Shendi provided fresh news from Cairo. He learned that Murad Bey had surrendered to the French, but had fallen victim to the plague before he could undergo the humiliation of actually fighting on their side. Ibrahim had long since escaped - to Istanbul it was said. In 1802, Maxim learned that the French had pulled out of Egypt the year before. By 1805, the incoming caravans brought the first news that the new Pasha of Egypt was a man named Muhammad Ali, an Albanian soldier who, with his ten thousand troops, had successfully resisted British attempts to gain control of Egypt. By 1807, news arrived that a steady stream of mamluks had begun trickling back into Lower Egypt, lured by reports that Muhammad Ali was a friend.

36

At first, Maxim felt no desire to join the mamluks returning to Cairo. There was much to occupy him where he was. He and the brothers had begun to experiment with new crops and new farming methods that he had heard about at Shendi and the results were promising.

The tribe had relocated twice in the last five years, moving further upriver. The first time, because the huts appeared to be in danger of collapsing from the weight of sand deposited against their windward side by the north easterly wind; the second time was because they burned down the huts: scorpions had infested the thatched roofs.

By the second move, Mayya had given birth to their second child, a curly-haired, light-eyed boy who the villagers treated like their own tribal mascot as he toddled about on his sturdy little legs, asserting himself over all and sundry and basking in the love and attention showered down on him. Maxim named him Arun and was totally captivated by him. Showing his affection for both his children came easily to Maxim and it did not escape his attention that as time went on, Mayya appeared to be more at ease inside herself. He wondered whether she was simply pleased at the bond that existed between him and his children, or whether her fear that someday he would return to his own kind had finally subsided. Either way, he was glad she was content because he could imagine no other life than the one he had created for himself here with her.

Gradually, however, with reports that the trickle of mamluks returning to Cairo had turned into a flood, Maxim's mind became preoccupied with thoughts of home. He wondered secretly whether in fact his father was really dead, or if he had somehow managed to stay alive. If Qilij had been somewhere safe in Cairo all these years and the recent rumours he had heard from the mamluks at Shendi

—that they were being welcomed back to Cairo—were indeed true, then possibly Qilij might have already taken up residence in his home once more and was perfectly safe. The thought that his father might still be alive and well began to prey on Maxim's mind and he woke up one morning knowing that the time had come for him to return home.

When he told Mayya of his decision she betrayed no surprise. It had occurred to him more than once that after all this time she could probably read his mind like a book. Like most marriages, their love making had settled into a routine interaction, comforting and comfortable, but from time to time, passion still ignited them. Last night had been one of those nights, and as he held her in his arms afterwards, the thought of being away from her seemed so unbearable that he almost regretted his decision to go.

"I will return before the next inundation," he promised.

"By then I will be a widow," was her calm reply.

"Do not speak such words," he said angrily.

"Then stay," she said simply. She turned to face him, her breath warm on his face.

"You know that this is something I must do," he said to her in the darkness.

"Then before you leave, give me another child," she said. And with that, she moved over him, straddling him with her legs, sinking down and down onto him and rocking her torso till he was so deep inside her, and the heat of their mutual passion so intense, that he could no longer tell where he ended and she began. Over and over, because she would not let him withdraw, his seed spilled hotly out of him deep in her belly, and they both knew, without any doubt, that Mayya had conceived that night.

A few days later he was ready to leave. The evening before his departure Noura had dissolved into tears when he told her he would be gone the next morning before she woke up and she had vowed to stay awake all night so she could see him leave. He promised to be away no longer than five full moons and that he would bring her something special from Cairo. But she would not be distracted.

"I just want you to come back," was all she said and he marvelled yet again at how discerning she was, how much like her mother.

Arun was more prosaic, merely asking Maxim to bring him a sword. Maxim ruffled his hair, laughing:

"I will, but it will be taller than you," he told Arun.

"How do you know that you will be back in five full moons," Mayya asked him later that night. "It is bad luck to make promises when it is not certain that you will be able to keep them. Noura will be worried when all the moons have passed and you are still not back."

"Do not worry. If my father is alive I will spend a little time with him and then set out for home," Maxim said confidently.

"And if he is not?"

"Then I will be back before you have even realized that I had gone," he said teasingly.

Mayya's face betrayed her anxiety that he should tempt the gods so frivolously, but she said nothing.

Maxim set out early the next morning, accompanied by two of his brothers-in-law who would stay with him until he sighted a caravan. At this time of year, a trip downriver was impossible, and the route through the desert he would have to travel was unfamiliar to him and dangerous. They travelled on horseback, with two camels loaded up with supplies of food and water. Just south of Assouan, they sighted a caravan and hastened to catch up to it. Once he had received the merchant's permission to join the caravan, the brothers wished Maxim a safe journey and turned back. He was on his way to Cairo.

37

Cairo, 1810

After the peace and quiet of his village, Cairo burst upon Maxim's eyes and ears anew in an explosion of light and sound so bright and so loud that for a moment, he fancied that the city was in the throes of some unusual occurrence. Then remembrance came flooding back; these were simply the sights and sounds of daily life in Cairo, no more and no less than when he had left it. Filled with nostalgia, he rode through the gateway and into the city from which he had been forced to flee so many years ago.

In the city he noted with mixed emotions the changes that Napoleon's brief sojourn had wrought. Some badly needed improvements had obviously been made, but at what price to his father, and others like him, he wondered uneasily? As he turned the familiar corner, he knew relief. His father's house was still standing, its exterior virtually unchanged.

With some trepidation about what might await him inside, Maxim dismounted from his horse and banged on the gate. At the sound of footsteps shuffling on the other side, he took a step back, tensed for the unexpected. Then the gate was opened a crack and joy welled up in his heart as the old doorkeeper's face appeared in the opening.

"Are you still sleeping on the job then, old man?" he asked. The smile in his eyes belied the sting of his words. The doorkeeper peered at him intently and then broke into a wide toothless smile:

"Praise be to Allah. He has delivered you home safely, master Maxim," he said, drawing a dingy piece of cloth from the folds of his tunic and wiping his eyes with it. He opened the door wide, at the same time shouting for the groom, who materialized in seconds and led the horse away, glancing curiously at Maxim.

Maxim crossed the courtyard quickly and bounded up the steps.

"Father?" he called. A chill of foreboding enveloped him as his voice echoed hollowly in his own ears. With quick steps he walked down the empty passageway and almost collided with Zainab.

"Thanks be to Allah you are indeed alive," she said quietly. "Your father has refused to believe otherwise all these many years."

"I too am glad to find you in good health," he replied. Her face was unveiled and Maxim's mind registered the fact that she had matured into a beautiful woman, one who could still turn a man's head. On instinct, his heart began to beat faster.

His expression must have betrayed his thoughts because she lowered her lashes.

Assuming that he had probably been staring and had made her uncomfortable, Maxim hastened to undo the damage.

"Forgive me," he said. "I did not mean to offend you. It is just that . . ." His voice trailed away with the realization that there was no way to explain, without offending her yet again, that the sight of her had affected him just as it had done all those years ago when he had gazed on her face for the first time, back there in the gloom of the engraver's shop.

She looked up at him again, her eyes luminous, but he thought he saw sadness in their depths and was moved by it.

"Do not apologize, Maxim," she said. "You have not offended me."

"Shall I take you to your father?" she inquired.

"Yes. Where is he?" he asked, grateful that she had changed the subject.

"He is waiting for you upstairs." She hesitated, looking at him uncertainly.

"What is it?" he demanded. "Is something wrong with him? Is he ill?"

"He is not . . . ill. But he is old and very, very tired. He has waited only to see you," she replied. Her meaning was clear.

"Then I shall go to him at once," Maxim said.

Qilij's eyes were fixed on the door and when he perceived Maxim standing in the doorway, they blazed with unaccustomed joy. Maxim moved to the side of his bed, took his father's hand and kissed it.

"I have missed you, Father," he said. "But these many years you have never been far from my thoughts."

"I knew you would come. I felt it," Qilij whispered. His voice quavered, so that Maxim had to lean forward to hear him.

"I would have come much sooner, Father, for I feared constantly for your safety. As soon as word arrived that the mamluks were free to return to Cairo, I hastened to your side and I will remain here with you."

Qilij moved restlessly and his fingers tightened their hold on Maxim's hand.

"Listen to me," he said, his voice becoming stronger with urgency. "Do not trust the Albanian. One who purports to be a friend to all is the most dangerous foe. He was friend to both Turks and mamluks while they struggled against each other after the British left Egypt. The Turkish governor clasped the Albanian viper to his bosom and felt the sting of his fangs. He seeks control of all Egypt and is supported by the sheikhs. The mamluks are now the only ones who may still rise again to thwart his ambition because although our numbers have decreased, we are still the feudal owners of the land. Ali cannot rule Egypt unless he breaks the mamluk hold on the land because it is the true source of Egypt's wealth and power. One day he will rise up against us and that day draws ever closer.

"Promise me," and Qilij's fingers clutched Maxim's hand like a vice, "promise me that as soon as I am buried, you will leave Cairo and return to where you came from, where you have been safe these many years."

"I promise, father, you have my word. But do not tire yourself with these thoughts. Rest now. I will remain by your side while you sleep and will be here when you awake.

We will talk of these things when you are stronger." Qilij, seemingly exhausted by his long speech, made no reply, but his fingers relaxed their hold slightly on Maxim's hand, although his eyes remained fixed on his face.

"Zainab," Qilij said suddenly. He seemed agitated once more.

"Yes, Father. Shall I get her for you?"

"No, no," Qilij said, his head moving restlessly on the pillow. "Take care of Zainab," he said. "She saved my life. When the soldiers came they put their guns to my head and she saved my life. Do you understand?" he demanded, his voice rising. His grip tightened anew on Maxim's hand and his eyes fastened on Maxim's, feverish and bright.

"I do, Father," Maxim said soothingly, unsure of what he was supposed to understand. "I am very grateful to Zainab for all she has done for you. I will ensure she is taken care of. Do not worry. Sleep now and we will talk again in the morning."

Qilij's eyes remained locked on Maxim's face and Maxim had the impression that there was something else he wished to say. But then Qilij's body relaxed and he gave a little sigh.

"You, and Arun, were the lights of my life," he said, and closed his eyes tiredly. Maxim remained where he was, his hand still clasped in his father's, until he was sure that he had fallen into a deep sleep. Then he withdrew his hand, pulled the silken coverlet over his father, and seated himself in a chair at the side of the bed. Within minutes, exhausted by his long journey home, Maxim was fast asleep.

38

Maxim was awakened by that uncanny silence that denotes the complete absence of human presence and knew instantly that his father's soul had departed during the night. He knelt at the bedside and touched the cool brow tenderly.

"Joy awaits you in Paradise, my father," he murmured softly, grieving. But his grief held none of the bitterness that Arun's death had wrought. Qilij had lived his three score and ten, making his dying a seemly progression of his existence, whereas Arun's life had been cut short before it could be fulfilled. Even now, the blow still seemed too bitter to accept. Yet, to Maxim's surprise, he felt none of the loneliness that he had anticipated this moment would bring and it occurred to him that he no longer felt alone. Just north of Dongola there was a place that he now thought of as home.

The burial took place that same day. There were very few mourners. Many mamluks had returned to Cairo, but they were still reluctant to be seen congregating in large numbers and had even taken to wearing the galabiyah and shaving off their beards the better to blend in with the Egyptians. In any event, many of Qilij's contemporaries had preceded him in death or had been killed during the French invasion.

When Maxim returned from the funeral, he sought out Zainab.

"You have been the soul of kindness to my father," he said. "His house will be your home for as long as you wish."

"It is your father who was kind to me," she replied. "I am the one who is eternally grateful."

"What has become of Qualub and the women?"

"They are all dead. Qualub was killed by the French. One of the women died five years ago and the other last year after a long illness. I, too, was ill, and it was the khatbeh, my aunt, who restored me to health. She also was alone and although she is getting older she has been kind enough to remain here to keep me company and assist me in caring for your father. After the French came, the Egyptians, even the poorest peasants, could not be persuaded by any means to enter the house of a mamluk, for fear of being denounced as a traitor. So until very recently I could find no one who was suitable to work in your father's household. But my aunt is seeking other accommodation, now that you have returned."

"Pray inform her that she is welcome to remain," Maxim said hastily. "Once the three days of mourning have passed, and I have put my father's affairs in order, I will return to Nubia, where I have been since leaving Cairo." He did not elaborate but as Zainab looked at him he could see comprehension dawning on her face.

"How was it that my father's life was spared, and yours?" Maxim asked, after a little while. "I had understood that any mamluk who had not fled the city had been put to death by the French when they arrived, along with any who helped them. Did my father go into hiding?"

"No, he did not. He was too frail and would not have been able to withstand the difficulties." She paused before continuing. "The French soldiers did discover your father's presence in the house, but the women and I persuaded them that he was on his deathbed and therefore harmless."

Her eyes, large and almost black, were fixed on Maxim's face, but he had the impression that they looked past him into a void, and for a moment he was silenced.

"The French confiscated all mamluk property," Zainab then went on, "but your father had hidden away some of his reserves. He entrusted me with it to make expenditures necessary to support his household and I have kept scrupulous accounts. Naturally, there was no longer a pension. "

"That was to be expected," Maxim acknowledged. "I had heard of it and did wonder from time to time how my father would support himself if indeed he had survived. How have you managed since then?" he asked, looking at her curiously.

"My parents died and all their property passed to me. Their wealth was considerable. However, when the French imposed a requirement that all property held by Egyptians be registered and put in place a new system of taxes on buildings, my inheritance dwindled considerably and my parents' home which they had left to me was seized as payment in lieu of taxes. Nevertheless I did retain some money and it has been more than enough for my needs. My aunt pays her own way and is very astute. I depend on her to strike a good bargain when a purchase is needed."

"How was it that my father's house was not confiscated?" Maxim wanted to know.

"It was, along with all your father's remaining property. The soldiers came to look around and told us to begin packing our things. We prepared to go but possibly this house, being in the suburbs, was unsuitable for use as offices, because it was never occupied. Then too, the people began to riot in the streets because of the new taxes so I suppose the soldiers were kept busy trying to maintain law and order. It was fortunate for us that they did not need the house although, had we been forced to leave, my aunt the khatbeh offered us shelter in her home."

Zainab's voice had taken on a wooden quality, like someone who was now wearied, and Maxim looked at her intently. Something about her bothered him, but this time it had less to do with the attraction to her that had quickened again in him when he first arrived. All at once he recalled his father's agitation when he spoke of Zainab and how she had saved his life and his heart plummeted with intuitive dread. Maxim of all people knew what soldiers were capable of, whether French or mamluk. Even supposing that Zainab had anything left to bargain with for Qilij's life—and clearly she did not—men such as these did not bargain with women. They took them. Was it possible that what Qilij had tried to tell him—but could not bring himself to speak the words—was that the French soldiers had made an exception in Zainab's case: her body in exchange for Qilij's life?

At that thought, Maxim's mind hastily rejected any further consideration of the awful possibility that had just reared its ugly head because he sensed that for him, the

149

sure and certain knowledge that she had been raped would be an unsupportable burden. Since childhood Zainab had been in the periphery of his life. Arun had died because he, Maxim, had chosen to help her leave her husband. She was the woman who had awakened his sexuality: her face had kept him awake at night. She had looked after his father for ten years. And all along he had known in his heart that there was only one reason for everything she had done. She had done it because she cared deeply for him. He had never acknowledged it and now in some strange way he felt guilty, as though what he now strongly suspected had happened to her was his fault. So no, he did not want the certainty of truth and letting her know that he had guessed her terrible secret would serve no purpose. Forcing her to speak of it would only make her relive the horror and feel ashamed in his presence, even though she was blameless. In any event he had no doubt at all that he was the last person with whom she would want to discuss it. The only thing he could do for her now was to carry out his dying father's wish and protect her as best he could from further harm.

"I am greatly indebted to you for the way you have cared for my father," he said to her then, "and it is a debt that money can never repay. Nevertheless, whatever remains of my father's reserves is yours to keep." His voice was calm and very gentle, with no hint of the inner turmoil he was experiencing.

"I would not think of it," she declared vehemently. "I have more than enough to meet my needs. What remains of your father's reserves is completely at your disposal."

"Nevertheless, you were at his side, caring for him for ten years, and out of simple gratitude I would like you to have it," he insisted. "I myself have no need of a great deal of money, for I will not be remaining long in Cairo. My home is now elsewhere. "

"Then take it with you when you go," she replied. "The future may well be uncertain and it is all you have from your father." And she steadfastly refused to be persuaded.

"Very well," he said at last. "Let us speak no more of it for now."" And with that, the subject was closed.

150

39

Late that evening in Zainab's quarters

Zainab had lost count of the nights when she had lain awake reliving the horror of her experience when the three French soldiers had stormed into Qilij's house. The tenth of August, 1798. A date she would never forget. She felt doomed to relive that day over and over and strangely, instead of fading, the memory of it seemed to grow more vivid with the passage of time.

Now, as she prepared for bed, Zainab was wearily conscious that once again she was engaged in her struggle with memories that refused to be permanently suppressed. There had been too many nights when the effort of keeping her thoughts at bay would keep her awake all night. Tonight, she knew she would lose again. The heavy footsteps of the soldiers tramping through the courtyard and into the house were already resounding in her brain.

Her first thought was that the whole French army had invaded the house. The screaming of the women had brought her rushing from her quarters and she arrived in the harem just as one of them, his pistol cocked and pointed directly at Qilij's head, seemed on the verge of firing.

"No!" she screamed. He turned, his pistol pointed in her direction. "No, please, no! He is old and harmless. There is nothing he can do to hurt you. He will not live long enough. I beg you please, if you must kill, kill me instead."

"Taisez-vous, donc!" the soldier shouted, and even though they spoke no French the two old women understood him instinctively. Their high-pitched wailing tapered off abruptly into groaning whimpers.

"Bon! Now, what are you saying?" the soldier said, speaking in French. Zainab spoke no French, but somehow she understood the question and forcing down her fear, she endeavoured to communicate with him in pantomime.

"She wants us to take her instead," the soldier said laughingly to his two comrades, misinterpreting Zainab's message. He returned his pistol to its holster. "I think this is a good offer, n'est-ce pas? Le vieux n'est pas du tout dangereux. But she is too pretty to shoot. And we have been away from France too long. Keep watch, and do not allow any of the others to enter. If the old one moves, shoot him," he said carelessly.

"Viens, ma belle," he said to Zainab, seizing her arm in a grip of steel and leading her out of the room. "Let us find some more private accommodations."

Panicked with the realization that her offer had been horribly misunderstood she began to struggle, her mouth opening in a scream. But it was too late. He dragged her through the first door he came to, which was the door to her own quarters, flung her down on the divan and fell heavily on top of her, pinning her down with his knee while he unbuttoned his breeches.

After a while, she didn't struggle any more, not even when his two comrades entered one after the other and took their time raping her.

When the soldiers finally left, the two old women, frightened almost to death, had crept into the room and cleaned her up. Her body felt limp, as though she were unconscious, but her eyes were wide open, staring at nothing. Finally, after two days had passed with no outward sign of response from her, one of them had crept out and when she came back, the khatbeh was with her.

Gradually, after many days, as her mind allowed itself to leave that safe and secret place to which it had retreated, she began to respond to the khatbeh's ministrations. Time passed and she resumed the motions of living, but inside, she felt completely dead, no hate, certainly no love: a complete absence of emotion.

"Do it!" she said dispassionately to the khatbeh, when she realized that she had conceived a child. And it had been done. Wracked by unbelievable pain, the sweat pouring out of her body, she had clenched her teeth, refusing to scream. She had bled profusely, more than seemed possible without bleeding to death, she thought absently, before lapsing into unconsciousness. On the third day, her fever subsided and the khatbeh was there when she opened her eyes.

"You will live," the khatbeh said, stroking her brow.

"That is unfortunate," she replied, and closed her eyes.

For many months, she had lived in terror that the soldiers would return, but they never had. Perhaps they were too afraid that Bonaparte would discover they had disobeyed his orders that the Egyptian women were not to be touched. She knew relief only when word came through the grapevine that Napoleon had ordered that one hundred prostitutes be sent to Egypt from France, for the soldiers' use. The house was never again searched, and Qilij had remained in safety.

The death of the two women brought Zainab another measure of relief: the certainty that now her story was safe. Her aunt would never betray her secret and Maxim would never know the high price she had paid for his father's safety. She had reflected many times that Arun had given his life for her, and now she had given hers to save Qilij. For the thousandth time, as she lay in bed that night staring into the darkness, she cursed fate drearily for not completing the transaction and allowing her body to die, just as her heart and soul had died on that terrible day.

Gone, too, was the girlhood dream, long secreted in her heart, of a life lived fully and completely, secure in the affection of the only man she had ever cared about and surrounded by the children she would have borne him: Maxim. Throughout the miserable years of being Khalid's wife and the beatings she had endured, she had clung to that dream, knowing all the while that it was impossible because Khalid would have killed her rather than let her go. In her desperation she had turned to Maxim for help and he had rescued her. That was when she knew she had always been right about him and that for her there would never be anyone else but Maxim.

She had almost become undone today by the look in Maxim's eyes when he saw her because it had come too late. What the French soldiers had done to her had left her feeling unclean and empty inside. She was no longer worthy of him. Whatever he might feel for her now would quickly turn to pity if he ever found out the truth, and that she could not bear.

40

As the mourning period drew to a close Maxim became restless and began preparing himself mentally for the long journey back home. He longed for the peace and comfort of body and mind that awaited him there. Cairo had lost the appeal it once held for him. Qilij had passed on and whatever might once have been possible between himself and Zainab, was no longer so. He still thought her beautiful, but her eyes were dark and bottomless wells, without the faintest spark of life, a tragedy of expressionlessness that pained him to see. Unable to change the past, he could only move forward: go on with the life fate had mapped out for him.

Late one afternoon, seized with boredom, he rode out of the city and up into the Muqattam Hills. Finding a sheltered spot in the face of the cliff, he dismounted from his horse and stood looking out over the escarpment, entranced anew by the magic and mystery of Cairo. Partly shrouded under the late afternoon haze, the city exuded all the romance of The Arabian Nights' Entertainments, her domes and minarets emerging from the shroud of mystery to dot the landscape with their ornate mysticism, mute testimony to man's desire to escape from the mundane, to lift his eyes upward and connect to a higher power.

A horse whinnied softly nearby and Maxim turned sharply to perceive a man standing about fifteen feet away, holding the reins of his horse. He seemed to have materialized out of thin air and Maxim's surprise at his sudden apparition gave way almost immediately to suspicion tinged with annoyance.

"Who are you? Show yourself!" he commanded.

"A thousand pardons. I did not mean to startle you."

"You have not answered my question," Maxim replied, his voice still betraying annoyance.

"I saw you approaching and withdrew into the shelter of the cliff until I could determine whether you were friend or foe. Like you, I merely sought a quiet place." His voice was mild. "May I approach so that we may speak more softly? My voice grows weary."

Maxim nodded curtly and the stranger moved forward, closing the gap between them to about five feet. He was a small, spare man, shorter than Maxim, with light brown skin, a reddish beard generously sprinkled with grey and eyes that made Maxim suddenly think of his old enemy, Baltaa.

"You must be a stranger here," the man said, his eyes penetrating.

"Why do you say that?"

"I observed you as you looked out over the city. You do not take the beauty of Cairo for granted. That luxury is reserved for those who, surrounded by it daily, have become immune to it."

"I am a stranger, of sorts," Maxim admitted, feeling more at ease. "The city was my home during my youth, but I have been away from it for ten years now."

"You wear the galabiyah, yet I doubt that you are Egyptian."

"I was born on the Russian steppes, but until recently, knew no other home but Cairo."

"You are a mamluk?"

"Yes."

"What has brought you back here?"

"You ask many questions, for a stranger. I find your interest in me somewhat perturbing, since I do not know who you are, although I also doubt that you are Egyptian."

"My name is Mehmet Ali. I am Albanian. Do not be alarmed," he continued in a reassuring voice, as Maxim started visibly. "I am aware that several of your kind have returned to Cairo and I plan to seek their commitment to join forces with me in leading Egypt into the future. All are welcome here."

The restless eyes fastened suddenly on Maxim's face. "What was your purpose in returning after such a long absence?"

"Mainly to discover whether my father, my benefactor, still lived."

"And?"

"I buried him only four weeks ago."

"What are your plans now?"

"Now that my father has passed on, I will return to Nubia."

"You no longer feel any attachment to Cairo?"

"Very little," Maxim replied. "The mamluk way of life holds very little appeal for me now. In any case, it is an era whose time has passed. A new world awaits at Egypt's doorstep and our presence here may prove to some an unwelcome reminder of the past."

"You speak the language of the intelligent. I will have need of men like you, for to tell you the truth, the task of preparing millions of Egyptians for the changes that the next few decades will bring is a formidable one, given that their thinking has remained unchanged for centuries. You should give some thought to remaining here a little while longer."

"You flatter me," Maxim said.

"Not in the least. Consider, if you will, the question of obligation. Now may be the time for the mamluks to repay Egypt for all that they have received—and taken—from her, by sharing in the work that needs to be done. Do you see?"

"The mamluks have never burdened themselves with matters of conscience, and in that, I am as guilty as the others," Maxim smiled. "However, I find your words intriguing, and I will think on the matter. In the meantime, darkness falls and we should make our way down in safety while some light remains."

"Perhaps we will meet again."

"I should find that most agreeable," Maxim replied and mounting his horse, he made his way carefully down, followed by Ali. As he rode through the gates of the Citadel Mehmet Ali lifted his hand in silent farewell and Maxim continued on his way home.

Over the next few days, the surprising encounter was never far from Maxim's thoughts. The man who had introduced himself as Mehmet Ali was none other than Muhammad Ali, the man whom his father had warned him not to trust. It was difficult to reconcile the image of a man who spoke of duty and obligation and of leading Egypt out of the dark ages with the treacherous image of Muhammad Ali conjured up by his father. The challenge of building a new Egypt appealed to Maxim personally and he felt torn between that and the desire to return to his family. Of the two choices, the allure of fame that would clothe the one who influenced the destiny of Egypt was by far the more dazzling prospect.

41

Maxim had spoken to no one of his encounter with Muhammad Ali: there were none in whom he felt he could confide. But as he wrestled with his thoughts, Zainab observed him and attributing his air of abstraction to a totally different reason, she sought out her aunt.

"Maxim grows restless," she said to her. "I do not believe that he is still celibate and perhaps he feels the need for the comforts of the harem?"

The khatbeh understood her question immediately, and her eyes lit up at the prospect of being once more openly engaged in the business she loved so well. "I will make discreet enquiries," she said. "I take it there will be no difficulties regarding price?"

"None, for the right girl." Her voice sounded dull, and the khatbeh looked at Zainab with sudden concern.

"Are you sure that this is your wish?"

"Yes, aunt. Do not trouble yourself about my feelings, for I assure you, I have none. We will settle the account, you and I, when you have found a suitable girl," she said. She stood up and kissed the khatbeh's cheek. "Goodnight, aunt."

42

Maxim kicked the silken covers off his divan. In the late summer heat he now found them suffocatingly soft and he longed for the cool firmness of the rush mat on which he had spent so many comfortable nights. He had not yet forsaken the habit he had adopted from the villagers of going to bed as soon as the sun had disappeared from view and rising with the first streaks of early dawn. But tonight, for some reason, sleep was long in coming and finally he gave up the effort and got up. It would be more agreeable to sit in the qa'ah, because it faced north and was open to the cooling winds.

As he walked down the passageway, the sound of singing drifted past his ear. He stopped, trying to determine where it could be coming from, and who the singer could possibly be. He dismissed the thought immediately that it could be either Zainab or the khatbeh. He couldn't imagine either of them breaking out in song. As the singing continued, he realized that it could only be coming from the harem and he retraced his steps and mounted the stairs.

Approaching the harem he stopped, peered through the mashrabiya, and was transfixed by the vision that greeted his eyes. There, lying amongst a heap of silken cushions, was the most beautiful creature he had ever seen. As he watched, she stopped singing, sat up and yawned delicately, transparently bored. She was dressed in gauzy pantaloons of some yellowish material, and was nude above the waist, except for her hair, the colour of a blood moon, flowing over her shoulders to cover her breasts. As though aware of being observed, she raised her arms and lifted her hair away so that it cascaded down her back, exposing creamy pubescent breasts. Her nipples were a daub of pale pink, like the final touches of an artist's brush.

160

At the sight of them, Maxim felt a stirring in his groin. Embarrassed lest anyone should approach and perceive him in such an obvious state of sexual excitement, he abandoned his intention to enjoy the cool night air in the qa'ah. Instead, he retreated to his room and threw himself on the bed.

The girl was obviously destined for him but the realization was accompanied by a shrinking feeling that this was probably the work of Zainab's aunt, the khatbeh. Years ago she had offered him her services as a betrother. His refusal had been curt. Although still very young his head had been filled with lofty ambitions then and a determination to outdo the other soldiers, to be the best. Youthfully idealistic, he had been a little offended by what the khatbeh's offer seemed to imply: that he was not at all exceptional, that he was no different from the others, that without a woman he was somehow incomplete. Later, he had heard rumours that she was making inquiries about him, as to whether he preferred young boys, since he was constantly surrounded by them. He had laughed off the rumours. Certainly men had approached him, directly as well as in an oblique fashion, but no soldier had ever shared his bed at night. He knew the khatbeh provided her matchmaking services to some of the finest families in Cairo and had many ears that listened for her in the best houses, but he was confident they would have nothing to report.

The old crone was persistent, he'd give her that much. He'd been gone for years but the minute he returned there she was, back on the job again. Nevertheless, he had to concede that for her this was the way things had always been, how they should be. Men needed wives and since women could not be approached directly, an intermediary was required. Men also needed concubines and the khatbeh was more than willing to do the negotiating for that too. It seemed she had no intention of letting him slip through her grasp. She must have been extremely well paid for her services. She had been at it even before he was born and would probably still be bargaining with her last breath, he thought with cynical amusement.

His mind insisted on returning to the girl he had just seen. She was exquisite. The khatbeh had surely outdone herself this time. The thought that the girl was there for his pleasure was hard to resist. Lately, alone in his bed at night, being without Mayya had become increasingly difficult. He missed the welcoming warmth of her body, the way she filled his every need. He had never given any thought to seeking release elsewhere, although it was not uncommon among her people for a man to take a second wife. Mayya had always been enough for him. More than enough actually, since when he thought about it, he couldn't imagine being without her. She had saved his life, creating a bond between them that had been cemented by the years they had spent together as husband and wife and the children she had borne him: a bond that felt indissoluble.

But for several weeks now he had been conscious of a need inside him, growing stronger with each passing day, seeking outlet in the wet dreams that disturbed his nights. The sight of the girl must have crystallized that need because he was suddenly fevered with wanting. It was elementary and instinctive, unbound by either past, present, or future: an entity in and of itself that had seized him in its unrelenting grip. He knew it would not let him go until it had been assuaged.

He passed the night tossing and turning, resisting the urge to simply leave his bed and go to the girl, put an end to the searing hunger inside him. He breathed through his mouth in a futile attempt to expel the heat of it while he tried to think. There was likely some established protocol to follow in these matters, he reasoned. He just had to find out what it was. The khatbeh would not have brought the girl here without Zainab's permission so the only person who could enlighten him regarding procedure would be Zainab herself. Nevertheless, he cringed with awkwardness at the thought of approaching her.

The long night finally ended and he had never in his life been so glad to see the dawn. When the servant brought his breakfast he asked the woman to convey to Zainab his request that she meet him in the mandara in one hour.

He ate quickly and as soon as the hour had passed hastened to the mandara. Zainab was already there, waiting. After a few minutes of polite conversation, he broached the subject.

"The girl in the harem," he said, his voice carefully neutral, "when did she arrive?"

"Only yesterday. My aunt, who, as you know, is a khatbeh, took charge of all the arrangements. Do you find the girl pleasing?"

"Very much so, but I am unfamiliar with the custom in these matters. With whom should I now discuss the matter of price?"

"The circumstances are somewhat unusual," Zainab replied. "The child's father is of course unknown, except for the fact that he was a mamluk." Zainab paused momentarily and Maxim divined that the mother had most likely been taken by force. He looked away in momentary embarrassment, his eyes returning to Zainab as she continued to speak.

"My aunt knew the mother and when the child was born she advised the mother that because of the unfortunate circumstances of the girl's parentage, her only chance for a good life was to place her in the harem of a wealthy man. Observing the child's great beauty my aunt paid the mother in advance to keep her veiled and confined to the house while she trained her for her future duties. The girl is fertile and the khatbeh has confirmed that she is untouched.

"Do not be embarrassed, Maxim," she continued evenly. "It is customary for the women of a household to initiate these discussions on behalf of male family members and as you were preoccupied with grief I took the liberty of acting on your behalf. It is your right to do as you see fit in these matters. Even the poorest of Egyptian males may keep a harem if he is able to do so. If upon inspection you do not wish to keep the girl she will be returned to her mother. Shall I send her to you now so that you may inspect her?"

"No, no," Maxim responded hastily. "I thank you for acting on my behalf and do not foresee any impediments; however, I have a business matter to attend to in the city

and must leave almost immediately. I will visit the harem
when I return."

"As you wish," Zainab said. "She will be awaiting your
pleasure," she added, as she went out of the room.

By mid-afternoon Maxim had returned home. He had
spent most of the morning at the registry office making
inquiries as to whether it would be possible to repurchase
his father's house which was now in the possession of the
state but had gotten nowhere. Despite his frustration, all
morning he had been aware of the undercurrent of
electricity surging through his body in anticipation of what
awaited him at the house. Excitement quickened his
footsteps as he entered the house and rushed to his room
to change from his street clothes. One minute later he
emerged, hastily fastening a beautifully embroidered royal
blue tunic over his white silk pantalons, charged down the
hallway and took the stairs to the harem two at a time.

An expression of relief flitted over the girl's face when
he appeared in the doorway. As he entered the room she
went quickly toward him, seized his hand and led him over
to the divan. He sank down on it as she pirouetted in front
of him, seeking his approval; he could tell from her manner
that she was confident it would be forthcoming.

"You are a very pretty creature," he said to her with a
smile. Desire gnawed at him with its sharp teeth and he
suppressed it, suddenly wanting to savour the moment of
fulfillment now so close at hand.

"What is your name and how old are you?"

"I am called Zenobia and I am thirteen, master, but I
have developed very well for my age."

"Yes, you have," he agreed, amused. "Are you happy to
be here?"

"Very happy, master. And even more so because I
thought you would be old but you are not." He laughed
outright at that. She was charming and obviously not the
least bit afraid of him.

"You will not become homesick?" he asked

Her green eyes widened. "Oh no, master," she replied.
"No one would be homesick in such a beautiful house. I am
most fortunate to have been chosen by a family such as

yours. I would be very sad to leave here. And I have grown fond of you already."

"You have?"

"Of course, master. You are most handsome and I would find much pleasure in doing things that make you happy."

"What kinds of things?" His voice was husky, shredded from his self-imposed restraint that was about to disintegrate.

"I can make Turkish coffee, I can sing and dance for you, and I can pleasure you, master," she replied, and she moved forward and placed her hands caressingly on his chest. She spoke the truth, and from then on, it was a rare evening when he did not enter the harem.

43

Since his first encounter with Muhammad Ali, Maxim had twice gone back to the Muqattam Hills and was disappointed on each occasion not to find him there. He allowed several more weeks to pass before trying again. This time Muhammad Ali was there.

"I am pleased that you are not yet returned to Upper Egypt," Ali greeted him.

"Your vision of a new Egypt intrigues me greatly. I therefore delayed my departure in the hope that I might learn more of it from you," Maxim replied.

"Is it because the idea of greatness fascinates you?"

"Egypt has known greatness since the time of pharaohs but its splendour has long since vanished. How can we hope to rebuild Egypt when the two things which are key if she is even to survive are the very things on which one can least depend?"

Ali looked at him keenly. "And what are those?"

"The waters of the Nile and the peasants."

"Ah! What a pleasure it is to speak with one so intelligent."

"Then you agree?"

"I agree that those are the two things that we must seek to change. Not only are they necessary to her survival, they are the foundation on which the new Egypt will be built."

"You speak of change. How will this come about? Perhaps the peasants may be forced to change, but how will you command nature. The Nile obeys no mortal."

"That is very true, and Egypt has been at her mercy throughout history. Some years she overflows, turning the country into a lake; other years, she is capricious and allows the crops to perish. We cannot continue to leave our destiny in the hands of fate. When the Nile gives too much, there is a way to harvest it for those years when she gives too little.

"Look over there," he said, pointing north of Cairo. "If we build a dam there, when the Nile overflows, the water level in the dam will rise higher and higher, so that even in years of low Niles, there will be enough water to irrigate the fields continuously throughout the year, not just in August and September."

"And it will be possible then to cultivate the fields all year round," Maxim said eagerly.

"Exactly. The dam will also trap the silt brought down by the Nile, which can then be spread over a much larger area. We can cultivate not only wheat, but cotton, rice, even potatoes and the cane that provides sugar. Our export markets will be without limits."

"But the peasants have always resisted new ideas," Maxim said, "particularly if it means they must spend longer hours toiling in the fields. And that is what you are proposing."

"That is because they do not profit fairly from the fruits of their labours. All that will be changed. Then those who are still reluctant to work with the hoe will be conscripted to carry a gun. All must contribute to the building of the new Egypt, in one way or another. Egypt must become strong on all fronts."

"Your words are inspiring. But where is all this knowledge to come from. Dams cannot be built through reciting the Qur'an."

"We will begin by using the knowledge that has been left to us inside the brains of the French officers who did not follow Bonaparte back to France. They will help us build our schools and our factories; they will teach us what they know. They are bored and will jump at the chance. Once we begin, more of them will return from France, you will see. In the end, Egypt will once again surpass even France itself in greatness."

His voice was the voice of a visionary and as it rang out over the escarpment, it seemed to Maxim that all the citizens of Cairo must surely hear it and rush out of their homes to begin without delay the task of turning into reality the dream of greatness that he had laid out before them, a dream that Maxim himself now believed in fully.

He began riding frequently into the Hills and more often than not, Muhammad Ali would be there, waiting for him. Together, they honed the dream, in which Egypt took its place as a great, the greatest, world power. They fashioned a civilized, cultured society with centres of learning to which citizens of every other nation would flock in large numbers, a society that had not only freed itself from the yoke of the Ottoman Empire, but had taken control of it. As he outlined his vision, Muhammad Ali's face would become transformed and Maxim, watching, was spellbound by the hypnotic light emanating from his eyes.

44

Frequently, on returning home from his meetings with Muhammad Ali, instead of going into the harem, Maxim would retreat to his own room. Zenobia was still the charming pretty little creature whose seductive wiles were well-nigh irresistible, but sometimes he felt a pressing need to escape from her constant juvenile prattle that made sober thought almost impossible. He began to recollect Mayya's quiet intensity; her ability to sense his needs even before he could express them and a tight little knot of longing lodged itself in the pit of his stomach and took root.

One evening, as he entered the harem, Zenobia was lying face down on the divan, sobbing heartbrokenly. Dismayed, he rushed into the room and sitting down beside her, lifted her up into his arms. She continued to sob, burying her face in his chest.

"What is it, my pretty one? Why are you crying?" he asked, stroking her hair.

She lifted her face to look at him, streaks of kohl running down her cheeks. "You do not want me anymore, master. I am afraid you will send me back to my mother. Please let me stay here with you," she said, between sobs.

"Hush, you silly child," he said. "I am not going to send you back."

He could see that her distress was genuine and he felt a stab of guilt, remembering that several nights had passed since his last visit.

"I have been kept busy these past few days with other matters, but see, I am here tonight, am I not? Here," he said, withdrawing a fine linen handkerchief from his tunic, "wipe your face and let me have one of your pretty smiles. I have brought you a present. Look!"

And reaching into his pocket he drew out a necklace of gold, thanking his lucky stars that, pricked by his conscience, he had indeed thought to purchase it for her earlier that day.

She took it with a gasp of pleasure, draping it around her hand to better admire it. "Oh master," she breathed. "This is the most beautiful thing I have ever seen." She passed it back to him and lifting her hair away from her shoulders, she turned her back to him so that he could fasten it around her pretty neck. He did so and kissed the back of her neck:

"You see," he said, "even though I was not with you, you were in my thoughts."

"I am indeed a silly girl, master," she said, turning around to face him. She stood up and with a quick movement of her hands, unloosed her pantaloons and stepped out of them. Once again her beauty struck him anew and he felt himself quicken. He held out his hand and she knelt down beside him.

After his passion had been spent, she sat up. "I have something to tell you," she said, smiling shyly.

"What is it?"

"I think I am with child, master." Her expression was both anxious and proud. His heart lurched uncomfortably and he drew her back down to lie beside him, so that she would not see his face.

"Are you pleased?" she asked.

"I am pleased if you are," he said evasively.

She sat back up again abruptly and turned to face him. "Oh no, master!" she protested. "It is you who must always come first. What I feel is not at all important. If this is not what you want then you must send me away."

She sounded so earnest, so convinced; he realized that for her, being a concubine was a vocation, one she took seriously. She was barely thirteen so he imagined her training must have begun very early in life, possibly around the age of seven. It occurred to him then that this girl was not a great deal older than his own daughter, Noura, who would soon be ten. In just a few years a husband would have to be found for her. Most likely Mayya was already thinking about that, thinking ahead, teaching her daughter from early on the things she would need to know to care for her husband properly. Maxim felt his chest constrict at the thought that the day was not so far off when his daughter, his first child, would be gone from him and he experienced a painful sense of loss. He knew then that despite the fact that Qilij had not been his biological father, he had become exactly like him. He loved his children, all of them, including the child that Zenobia was now carrying. With this thought, he drew her back down to lie next to him.

"I have no intention of sending you away," he said. "After it is born you and the child must stay here, where you will be cared for."

Her body became very still and she did not immediately reply.

"When you go away, master, will you ever come back?" she asked

He glanced down at her in surprise.

"What has made you think I am going away?" he wanted to know.

"I do not know," she confessed. "It is just something that I feel."

Now it was his turn to be silent as he pondered what to say to her.

"I have a family elsewhere, in Nubia" he said finally. "I have a wife, a daughter who is almost ten and a son who is three. I must return there to ensure they are safe."

"But why do you not bring them here to live in the harem, Master? I think we would be very good company for one another when you are busy."

A wry smile quirked Maxim's lips at the image of Mayya in the harem. He sincerely doubted she would consider it even for a moment.

"I do not know if they would want to come. They are used to their own way of doing things," he said.

"I do not know this place, this Nubia," Zenobia remarked. "Is it like the city of Cairo?"

"It is very different from Cairo," he told her. "The people live together in small villages on the river banks. Their homes are made of dried mud and the roofs are made from the branches of trees. They must work very hard all day long in order to survive. They grow their own food and what they do not need they take to sell in the market and must travel many days to get there. Yet they are content," he ended reflectively.

"It seems a very hard life," Zenobia commented. "I think your family would be much happier if they lived here with you because they would be living in a great and beautiful house instead of one made of earth, they would not have to work and their feet would not be always covered in mud. And also, you would not have to travel there to see them. It is a long journey, is it not, master?"

"That it is," he admitted. "And a dangerous one."

He understood completely how her mind was working. If he returned to his family in this Nubia it was possible he might never come back and her security would be in jeopardy. If, on the other hand, he brought his family here, she and the child would still be under his protection. To protect herself and the child she was carrying, she had weighed her options and chosen the lesser of two evils: better to share him with his wife than to have no security at all. She was a child, but an oddly mature one, he mused, thoughtful and clever but still vulnerable. He observed her with renewed tenderness and resolved to do all in his power to protect her and his unborn child.

She sighed and then emitted a little yawn.

"If she comes, your wife will be the first wife of the harem, master," she said sleepily. "I promise I will be very obedient and helpful to her. I still have much to learn."

And with that her eyelids fluttered and stayed closed. She was fast asleep.

He waited a few minutes, then disengaged himself without awakening her and returned to his room. He threw himself down on the divan and after a few moments, sat up again, leaning against the wall, thinking about his predicament. Fathering children by two different women was commonplace, except that in his case, the two women were worlds apart. He was well aware that for many of his contemporaries, a Dongolawi woman might not have even entered into the equation, but he knew himself to be inextricably linked to Mayya.

Thinking of Mayya made him feel guilty for having left her to care for Noura and Arun on her own. His guilt worsened at the thought that she was carrying another child: there was no doubt in his mind that she had conceived on their last night together. He was aware that she would not really have to struggle alone: she would have as much help as she needed and more. In the Dongolawi culture the raising of a child was the responsibility of the village as a whole and it was taken seriously – that was their way of life. All the same he was plagued by the uncomfortable notion that simply by not being there he was failing his family and it was exacerbated by his feeling lately of being pulled in two different directions.

This new development with Zenobia was forging yet another link in the chain of destiny that threatened to encircle him and cut him off forever from his family. His unexpected meeting with Muhammad Ali had deepened into a friendship that had renewed his attachment to Cairo. Maxim's reason for returning was to find out whether his father was still alive. Allah had granted him the gift of seeing Qilij one last time and once his father had passed on he should have set out for home immediately. But fate had intervened again and now there lay before him a new opportunity to realize the goal that had always fuelled his endeavours: to excel as a leader. It beckoned like a golden road and he teetered indecisively on its edge, knowing that once he set foot on it he might never be able to retrace his steps.

He lay down again, looking up at the ceiling and its ornate pattern slowly dissolved before his eyes, replaced by the woven palm fronds of his hut. He closed his eyes and the scent of Mayya was everywhere.

45

From that day onwards, he resolved to be more conscientious in his duty towards Zenobia and he made it his business to visit the harem regularly, deliberately putting his thoughts on hold. She appeared to be delighted each time he came, but in spite of her heavily rouged face, he could see that she was becoming very pale.

"The girl seems very listless," he remarked to Zainab one day as they completed the accounts which she had insisted he review each month.

"The midwife, who attends her every morning, believes that her difficulty stems from the fact that she is very young and her body not strong enough to carry the child to full term comfortably. As she is in the third term of her confinement the midwife has agreed to move into the house so that she will be close by if she is needed suddenly. She will be paid handsomely for the inconvenience," she added.

"I do not need to tell you that you have my permission to do whatever you think is necessary," he said, and Zainab nodded.

About three weeks later, Maxim was awakened by the sound of screaming, in which there was so much agony that for a moment, he felt paralyzed. Then he jumped out of bed and ran down the corridor just as Zainab came swiftly out of one of the rooms, closing the door behind her.

"What is it?" he said, almost shouting.

"The labour has begun and the birth will be very difficult. The midwife is with her. I have to go back in, for she needs my help. I only came out to reassure you that everything possible is being done."

He covered his ears with his hands as scream after agonized scream echoed through the house.

"Go back to your room, Maxim," Zainab said quietly. "There is nothing you can do." She touched his hand, opened the door to the birthing room and disappeared inside.

His hands still covering his ears, he turned and almost ran back down the passageway to his room. Entering, he threw himself on the bed face down, his arms crossed over his head and ears in an attempt to block out the sound of her screaming. But it was useless, and finally he got up again. Taking a blanket he went downstairs and out into the courtyard where the screams no longer reached him.

At dawn, Zainab came out to find him. She sat down beside him on the bench. The air was sweet with the scent of dew and they sat in silence for some time.

"The girl is dead," she said finally, "and the child with her. It could not be delivered. Her pelvis was too narrow."

He bent over and wept, his face buried in his hands. After a few moments, she touched his shoulder and went indoors.

Maxim remained where he was, tears streaming from his eyes as he grieved for the charming little concubine and his unborn child who had died with her. The thought of how Zenobia must have suffered left him anguished. Surely she had done nothing wrong to die so young and so painfully. He had become quite fond of her, all the while knowing that in his heart he could never have given up Mayya. Zenobia had taken care of his needs as a man; Mayya did that too, but through her he had also found a deeper and more fulfilling way to live. His attachment to her far surpassed his fondness for Zenobia.

His tears flowed afresh as he thought about the child. It was excruciating that now he would never know whether it had been a girl or a boy, never see its little face, hear its voice laugh and cry, talk and sing, and all of a sudden his loss seemed all the more insupportable because he was so far away from his own living children. He thought about his other child, the one he knew Mayya had conceived the night before he left. It would have been born by now. Fear overcame him then, that fate was punishing him in some way and would take Mayya and their third child away from him as well and he resolved to cut short his stay in Cairo and return to them as soon as possible.

Later that day, Zainab came to see him again as he sat alone in the mandara. "I thought you should know," she said. "I sent for the girl's mother and she has now arrived to take her body away. She will be buried this day. I have given her a generous sum to take care of the funeral expenses." He nodded, and she left him.

As the afternoon drew to a close, he rode up into the Muqattam Hills, his face set. Death, he suddenly felt, was with him constantly, waiting impatiently in the wings and he spoke to it: "Rejoice, ugly jealous one," he said softly. "Once again you have sunk your long teeth into flesh that was young and beautiful and released your maggots, but that is the last time I will give you that opportunity. Remain at my side till eternity, if you wish, but from this day forward, you will receive nothing from me but old bones." As he stopped speaking a sudden gust of wind sent dust swirling angrily around his feet.

46

"You seem pensive," Muhammad Ali said, as he approached.

Maxim did not immediately reply. His eyes were fixed on some distant point on the horizon.

"My concubine died in childbirth during the night," he said eventually.

"Ah!" was all Ali said, but his sympathy filled the silence and the bond between them was almost tangible. Then he spoke again:

"Was she attended by a midwife?"

"Naturally."

"What is done cannot be undone, but these tragedies are the price we pay for our backwardness," Ali said.

"What do you mean?"

"Childbirth should never result in death. Some of our traditions cause our people unnecessary suffering that physicians in Europe have long since learned how to relieve. Midwives have no such skills, but through false notions of modesty, we refuse to let our women be attended by male physicians who are concerned only with the saving of lives."

"Are you suggesting that our women should reveal their bodies to foreigners, even though they be physicians?"

"I am well aware that it will be many, many years before such a thing will be acceptable to our people. But we must look to Europe if we are to move forward. We must send our young people abroad to acquire the knowledge that Europeans have possessed for decades, if not centuries. I prophesy that the day will come when Egyptian doctors, trained in Europe, will attend our women in childbirth, not midwives.

"But let us leave this sad topic. I have a favour to ask of you, and perhaps this is a good time to ask it, for if you accept, it will take you away from Cairo for a short while and the distraction will perhaps be a good thing."

"Speak."

"I think the time has come to engage others such as yourself to join with us in the task that lies ahead. I want to extend the hand of friendship to others of your kind who have remained in Upper Egypt through unnecessary caution."

"What is it you wish me to do?"

"I want you to undertake a journey into Upper Egypt, at least as far south as Assouan, to carry my message of friendship to your people. I want you to say to them that they are welcome to return to Cairo as full participants in our endeavours. Let us make an occasion of it," he continued, as Maxim remained silent.

"On March first I am hosting a grand reception and banquet for my son Tusun who will shortly lead a small army into Arabia to put down the Wahhabi rebellion. I would consider it a sign of friendship and goodwill if you and your comrades would join me in honouring my son. March first seems a most auspicious date for it, do you not agree?"

"It is a fine date and your overture of friendship is a generous gesture; however, I fear that convincing the mamluks to accept such an invitation will be an extremely difficult task."

"My dear fellow, I have every confidence that if anyone can persuade them of my sincerity, it is you. What do you say?"

"Again, you flatter me; however, if it is your wish, I will undertake the journey."

"When you return, come directly to the Citadel. I will leave orders that you are to be shown in to my presence immediately. I will be anxious to hear whether your mission was successful."

"I will leave in two days," Maxim said. "The loss of my concubine and my unborn child is a heavy weight that burdens my heart and my mind and perhaps, as you say, the mission will provide a distraction of sorts from my grief."

Muhammad Ali clasped him by the arm, his eyes glowing brilliantly.

47

As he had promised, Maxim departed two days later,
accompanied by an honour guard of four of Muhammad
Ali's soldiers.

"Because you are my ambassador, not a courier," Ali
had said. "But even without the guards, your safety is
assured. I have established law and order in Egypt, so that
all who travel within her borders may do so in safety. None
will dare harm you."

Misgiving was written on Zainab's face as he took leave
of her.

"You have forgotten your father's warning," she said.

"What do you know of it?" he asked, curious.

"You forget that news travels with the speed of light in
Cairo. It is common knowledge that you spend much time
engaged in discussion with Muhammad Ali. Many have
seen you descending together from the Hills. I do not have
a good feeling about this mission, Maxim. Muhammad Ali
is a master of deception, and where that fails, he resorts
openly to cruelty. The basest peasant knows this," she
said, her eyes large with foreboding.

"What he has done he has been forced to do. I too had
my doubts in the beginning, but I am now convinced that
he seeks only the good of Egypt. Change, especially in a
place such as this, takes courage and determination"

She shook her head. "You were always an idealist," she
said. "I pray that your awakening will not be unduly harsh.
May Allah protect you, Maxim."

The mamluks, camping upriver, welcomed him into
their tents. But when he explained his mission, they
became withdrawn, their faces betraying doubt, and in
several cases their attitude towards him cooled. But his
powers of persuasion were considerable. He had learned at
the feet of the master. By the time he returned to Cairo, he

had earned their confidence and their promise to show good faith by their presence at the Citadel on March first.

As arranged, he rode to the Citadel to make his report to Muhammad Ali, who showed inordinate pleasure at the success of the mission.

"You will be well rewarded for your service to Egypt and to me," he said. "I have in mind to appoint you governor of one of the provinces of Upper Egypt, because I know that is where you wish to be. There is much to do up there. I firmly believe that the source of the Nile holds great treasure, and I am anxious to begin exploration. It will be reassuring to me to know that one as trustworthy as you is there to protect our interests. Rest assured, you have my undying gratitude," he said.

Maxim's journey into Upper Egypt, so close to the frontier of Nubia, had been an emotional one for him because the terrain through which he travelled reminded him so acutely of the little village that had been his home for ten years. Thoughts of his family had never been far from his mind and had it not been for his promise to report back to Ali on the success of his mission, he might well have just kept going, propelled by his desire to go home. The journey had made him realize that it was where he wanted to be. Fate had led him to the Nubians and his life among them had changed him.

Ali's vision had rekindled the fire of ambition that had fuelled Maxim's early years but he saw now that it was a blaze that would inevitably burn itself out, leaving nothing behind to sustain his soul. Mayya and the children, and their children in turn, would fulfill him all the days of his life. He would not give up the substance to grasp at the shadow.

Maxim's mind was now made up. As soon as he completed his mission and the mamluks had returned to Cairo, he would set out for home. But first, there was something else he needed to take care of and it was of this that he now spoke to Ali.

"If I may, I have a favour to ask," Maxim said to Ali.

"Anything, my dear fellow," Ali replied without hesitation.

"As you know, Bonaparte confiscated all the mamluk property when he took control of Cairo. All those properties, including my father's personal dwelling, have remained in the hands of the state."

"I am aware of that," Ali said, nodding, his eyes on Maxim's face.

"Before setting out for Upper Egypt I had visited the registry office to inquire about the possibility of repurchasing my father's house since the state does not seem to have any particular use for it; however, the officials were unable to give me an answer as to whether the house could be sold to me."

"If I appoint you as governor of one of the provinces, which is my plan, your accommodations there are assured and I need not tell you they will be quite luxurious," Ali said, sounding puzzled.

"The house will not be for my own use," Maxim replied quickly, "since I will not be living in Cairo. If I am able to purchase the house my intention is to immediately transfer it into the name of the woman who has been living there for the past ten years."

"What is she to you?" Ali said, curious.

"A good friend," Maxim replied promptly. "She is an Egyptian, well born, who came to live in my father's house many years ago and although she eventually inherited property from her own father, she lost it all on account of the new tax system imposed by Bonaparte. She took good care of my father right up to his death and I feel that ensuring that she always has a roof over her head is the least I can do. She has become like a sister to me," he added.

"That is very generous of you," Ali said, watching him keenly. 'You say the authorities could not inform you of procedures to be followed that will allow you to purchase the property from the state?"

"That is so," Maxim said.

"Leave it with me. I assume your father's house was in the mamluk quarter, so it will not be difficult to find the records. I do not foresee any complications in returning the house to your name so that you can then transfer the title to this woman and have it registered in her name. Be at the registry office tomorrow at noon. You have my promise that the papers will be ready for you to sign. In view of the great service that you have rendered to me personally and to Egypt, the house will be my gift to you as an expression of my gratitude."

"I am overwhelmed by your generosity," Maxim said gratefully.

'Not at all, Maxim," Ali told him. "It is I who am in your debt."

Ali then escorted Maxim to the courtyard of the Citadel and in full view of all watching, kissed him warmly on both cheeks.

48

On March 1, 1811, Maxim rode out from his house, resplendent in a robe of brilliant blue. The day was gloriously bright, as though the sun itself sought to set its seal of approval on this auspicious occasion. Maxim was filled with enormous pride at what he had accomplished. It was a historic achievement and the apotheosis of the soldiering career upon which he had embarked so long ago. Finally, despite the ten-year hiatus, his dream of playing a pivotal role in leading Egypt to greatness was coming true. For Maxim, knowing that the change he was spearheading would be accomplished in a manner that did not involve bloodshed was gratifying. The events of his life had taught him that the satisfaction derived from killing another human being was by its very nature transitory and unsatisfying since enjoyment of the spoils was inevitably marred by the ever-present fear of retaliation by another. The peaceful change that he had been instrumental in initiating today would be permanent, recorded forever in the annals of Egypt's history.

Maxim felt that his whole life had finally come together, with no untidy loose ends. True to his word, Muhammad Ali had ensured the smooth transferral of ownership of his father's house and it was now registered in Zainab's name. Once this event was over and the work of rebuilding had commenced, Maxim planned to return home and then take up his new appointment as a provincial governor. Already, he envisioned everything that he would accomplish in this new role, establishing order and working towards expanding the industrial experiments of which Ali had spoken so eloquently to encompass villages as far away as Upper Nubia. He would be instrumental in bringing prosperity to his village and to his family.

Suffused with pride and happiness and entranced with his vision of the future, Maxim rode to the city gates, where over five hundred splendidly attired mamluks were already assembled and led them triumphantly through the streets of Cairo to the Citadel.

Ali was seated on a dais at the far end of the banquet hall. As Maxim entered the room he rose and crossed the room to greet him.

"Welcome, my dear friend," he said, kissing Maxim on both cheeks. Then he and Ali and Ali's son Tusun stood aside next to each other, watching encouragingly as the mamluks poured into the banquet hall and took their seats at benches for two placed around the perimeter. In front of each bench and within easy reach was a low table groaning with baskets of assorted breads, cheeses, and faience bowls filled with olives, cucumbers, lettuce and onions. There were platters piled with an assortment of meats and serving dishes filled with lentils and chickpeas. Standing against the wall behind every bench were two female servers who moved forward as soon as each mamluk was seated and began filling the exquisite maiolica goblets on the tables with cold water for the guests to freshen their mouths. In the background female musicians picked out ancient melodies on the lute and lyre as the mamluks shuffled around finding places to sit.

Once all the guests were seated they began to partake of the feast laid out before them and a buzz of conversation filled the air. The music died away and was immediately replaced by drumming as scantily clad dancers made their way into the central space of the hall, their bodies swaying to the rhythm of the drums as the mamluks cheered them on. They were followed by acrobats performing daring feats that must have taken them a lifetime to perfect and the mamluks cheered even louder.

The banquet was a resounding success and at the end of it Ali rose. A silence fell as he began to speak.

"My friends," he said, "thank you for the honour you have bestowed on me by your presence here today. As you may know, my son Tusun will leave shortly on a military expedition to Arabia to quell the Wahhabi rebellion which has been allowed to exist for too long. I know that Allah will guide his hand and his sword because it is a righteous endeavour. The Wahhabis are a threat to Islam and to the security not only of Egypt, but to our empire.

"I say "our empire" because I want to assure you that you are indeed a part of it and the fact that you have come here convinces me that you are also ready for it to be so. Let us not look back. From this day on let us move forward together. Egypt needs your knowledge and your strength to rebuild. Welcome back. Today is the first day of our new beginning."

Ali's voice had risen inspiringly and as he concluded his speech, even those mamluks who had worn an air of reticence as they rode into the Citadel, were convinced that their suspicions had been completely unfounded. But none was happier than Maxim, for whom this event was the culmination of everything he had hoped for, the beginning of a new era in which the mamluks, because of his leadership, would play an important role in leading Egypt to true greatness.

The reception over, Maxim led the mamluks proudly out of the building, down the steep passage to the Bab al-Azab gate and stood there, waiting for the huge wooden doors to be opened. When the first shot rang out, his heart lurched sickeningly in his chest and his body went cold as though ice had replaced the blood in his veins. He knew instinctively what it signalled: that the unthinkable had already begun but for an infinitesimal moment of denial that lasted an eternity, his mind refused to acknowledge it. He turned and looked back and death was already everywhere, grinning horribly and dancing a macabre dance to the staccato sound of rifle fire that filled the air like a loud monochromatic symphony, each note punctuated by the discordant screams of horses and men as they crashed to the ground.

The horses' hooves skidded uncontrollably on the steep slope, made even more slippery by the blood that was turning the narrow passage into a slimy river of red, and they crashed into each other and fell down in a tangle of broken legs, their agonized neighing a counterpoint to the symphony of death. And now Muhammad Ali's soldiers, wanting more, threw away their rifles and jumped down from the walls above. Scimitars flashing, they waded into the passageway like butchers gone suddenly insane in a slaughterhouse.

Frenziedly, Maxim tugged at the reins, urging his horse around to force it back up the passageway since the way ahead was blocked by the gates and the panicked horse, bucking and leaping over the tangle of bodies, did its best to obey. But then, as if possessed of some natural wisdom, it turned back of its own volition and tried to forge ahead, skidding wildly while Maxim struggled to keep a tight hold on the reins. In a moment of delirium he was certain he saw Death waiting at the wall, grinning.

Just as it seemed that he must crash headlong into its evil face, the horse's hooves cleared the ground in a mighty leap and he was over the wall and down to the street below. The horse collapsed with an equine scream of agony as the impact smashed its four legs to pieces and Maxim narrowly escaped being crushed under the dying animal's body as he tumbled out of the saddle.

The citizens who had poured out into the streets to enjoy the colourful procession of mamluks riding through the city and had waited to see them depart from the Citadel were now fleeing in terror, pursued by the screams of dying men and horses, the acrid smell of gunpowder and the hot and heavy stench of blood that was now filling the air. Tearing off his ceremonial robe as he ran, Maxim followed them, darting down passageways and through alleys even as the sound of slamming doors and gates conveyed to him their message that they would not give him refuge.

Coming upon a donkey left unattended in the street he jumped on its back and spurring the animal mercilessly he rode it furiously out of the city until it dropped under him, dead from exhaustion. He fell off and began to walk, neither knowing nor caring to which point it had brought him. Facing the truth that it was his naiveté, nay, his stupidity that had cost so many of his comrades their lives was agonizing. He had arrogantly ignored his father's counsel as he lay dying and had led the mamluks to their deaths. As he walked, tears of anger and mortification streamed down his face with the realization of how completely he had been taken in by Ali's duplicity. He had foolishly placed his trust in him and had been ruthlessly betrayed.

Maxim walked for hours. He realized he had wandered into the desert and worn out, he collapsed on the sand. All around him was eerie silence, the air as still as though heaven itself were holding its breath, appalled at having witnessed such horror. Then the still air around him was pushed away on a breath as soft and as strong as a collective of angels sighing, and the wind began to blow, gently at first, like a warning. Somewhere in the recesses of his mind, he knew what this was and that he should find cover, but he was incapable of turning that thought into action.

"The khamsin! The khamsin!" a voice whispered urgently in his ear, but he still did not move. His lack of respect seemed to anger the wind. It became a gale, whipping up tornadoes of sand that tore at his face, billions of tiny pieces of glass intent on blinding him and stripping away every particle of skin. It howled and moaned as though enraged to find him still in its path. It filled his nose and mouth and ears and every aperture it could find with sand so fine it passed right through his clothing and grated on his body. It seemed driven by a fury that would not abate until it had buried him. Maxim was choking to death and he welcomed it.

"Maxim," a voice said in tender reproach and he knew it was Arun, but he did not answer because he wished for death and feared that Arun would only help him to live.

When Maxim opened his eyes the wind had stopped. He was sitting up, leaning against a wall, and a merchant was kneeling on one knee in the sand in front of him, looking into his face.

"Where am I?" he asked. Maxim's mouth felt gritty and he spat out a mouthful of sand. The merchant offered him water and he rinsed his mouth and spat again before taking a few sips.

"In the ruins of a temple. It protected us. It is a miracle you are alive. You came out of the desert like a ghost in the middle of the khamsin. No one has ever survived the khamsin in the open desert. You should have been buried alive."

"Would that I had," Maxim replied stonily.

"It seems it was Allah's will that you should live," the trader replied, scrutinizing his face keenly. "Perhaps your time has not yet arrived. Your journey continues and that may well be the purpose of our meeting."

"You are leading a caravan?"

"Yes. On the way to Shendi market. What is your destination?"

"I am on my way to Dongola."

"You are welcome to join the caravan."

"I cannot pay you. I escaped a slaughter of my people and have nothing to give you."

"You are safe with us," the merchant replied.

Maxim arrived at the village late one afternoon, having left the caravan and trudged on alone. The children spied him first and came running out, two of them his own. Shouting and laughing, they seized hold of his arms and legs and as he walked into the compound, the adults came out of their huts to see what the commotion was all about. He sat down on a bench and Mayya appeared. She shooed the children away and they scattered obediently, except for Noura who sat down next to him on the bench and began to stroke his face while murmuring comforting little sounds, and Arun who had seized Maxim by the legs and was clinging on tenaciously. Mayya stood before him, her eyes intuitive. His eyes looked back at her but they were focused inwardly, gazing at the horror of what he had brought down on his comrades. There was no need for him to say the words so plainly written on his countenance: that he would never return to Cairo.

Mayya laid her hand gently on his shoulder. "Stay here," she said. "I will bring you something to eat."

She remained standing in front of him, her hand still on his shoulder.

"You have another son," she told him. "I waited for you to name him so that there would be a reason for fate to

189

keep you alive. He is sleeping. By the time you have eaten he will be awake."

A long tremor passed through Maxim with the knowledge that what he had secretly feared—that fate would take this child away from him, too—had not come to pass. He took Noura and Arun by the hands and stood up.

"No," he said to Mayya. "I will see him now."

She nodded and the three of them followed her into the hut.

Epilogue

Although Maxim represents a character in Egyptian lore his sojourn in a Nubian village is drawn from the historical fact that when the mamluks were defeated by Napoleon in 1798, they fled south to Nubia to escape being killed. Many of them remained there in hiding and began new lives among the people. Mamluks in Egypt were predominantly of Kipchak (Turkish) and Circassian origin. As a result, the children (and their Sudanese descendants) born of the mamluks' cohabitation with Nubians would likely possess the genetic traits of their combined African and European ancestry, as evidenced in Maxim's children.

Acknowledgments

I am grateful to the many scholars of Egyptian history whose works I consulted. I would also like to thank Lawrence Knorr for welcoming me to Sunbury Press and my editor, Jennifer Melendrez, whose insight helped me to develop and complete the novel.

Made in the USA
Charleston, SC
02 April 2012